CONTENTS

SILVERHILLS' RESCUE

Silverhills Book 3

ALL THINGS WESTERN

By S. Cox

ThunderTree
Keeper Tyree
Sheriff Tyree
Reuben Hayes

By Sandra Cox

Westerns with Romantic Elements

Gwen Slade, Bounty Hunter
TumbleStar
Silverhills
Return to Silverhills

Time Travel Western Romance

Geller's Find
Montana Shootists
Sundial

Modern Day Shapeshifter Western Romance

Mateo's Law

Mateo's Blood Brother
Mateo's Woman

AND MORE

Romantic Suspense with a touch of Paranormal
The Crystal
Paranormal Romance
Tall, Dark and Undead

Romantic Suspense
Queen of Diamonds

Regency Romance
Miss Redmond's Deception

Young Adult
Minder

Anthologies
Parallels: Felix Was Here

Backlist
Shardai
Akasha
Makita
Odin Cats
Boji Stones
Flower Gardens and More

Rose Quartz
Black Opal

Retired
Vampire Island
Moon Watchers
Vampire Bay
Power Stones
Sunset
Ghost For Sale
Love, Lattes, and Mutants
Love, Lattes, and Danger
Love, Lattes, and Angel

ALL RIGHTS RESERVED

A TIP OF THE HAT TO

Beta Readers
D. K. Deters
D. L. Finn

Ideas Slinger
D. L. Finn

ARC-ers
Jacqui Murray
Joe Congel

IT Guru
Sonya Blanchard

DEDICATED TO

Western Romance Author D. K. Deters

CAST OF CHARACTERS

Silverhills' Ranch Folk
Alex O'Malley, Brandon Wade's wife
Brandon Wade, Alex's husband
Sarah Marie, Alex and Brandon's child, twin
Jon, Alex and Brandon's child, twin

Jeff Wade, Brandon's younger brother
Lisa Reiner-Wade, Alex's friend, Jeff's wife
Seb, Jeff and Lisa's baby

Maria, Alex's friend
Cookie, bunkhouse cook
Martha, cook and housekeeper, Cookie's wife
Missus Simms, seamstress
Sam, the blacksmith
Charlie, cowhand
Tony, cowhand
Jonas, cowhand
Ralph, cowhand

Mission Folk
Rosie, Bodie's aunt

Bodie, Rosie's nephew
Father Jon
Sister Marie
Sister Sarah
Manuel

Store-cantina owner
Willer

Comanchero
Thiago

Outlaws
Earl
Shifty Eyes

Animals
Dancer, Alex's black stallion
Eagle, Brandon's roan stallion
Mongrel, Alex's dog
The buckskin, mare

CHAPTER 1

July, 1874

The sun hit a blood-red horizon and shot upward in a crown of tangerine brilliance, hurting the eyes, lighting the trail from the top of the canyon to the ranch house like a beacon thrown across the sea.

The early July morning a warm one.

Dust rose as a horse trotted up. Jonas, a young cowhand, reined in his sorrel gelding beside the woman who stood on the veranda. "Rider coming."

"Is it Brandon?" Hand over her eyes, Alexandria O'Malley Wade strained to make out the narrow trail at the top of the foothill that her husband and their men would come galloping over when they returned from the trail drive. Her tan split-skirt rustled as she leaned against the smooth white-painted railing, trying to get a better view.

Jonas pushed up in his stirrups. Worn leather boots peeping from canvas chaps. "Can't tell."

The speck at the top of the canyon grew as it came tumbling down the trail. Her heart thumped and her breath lodged in her throat. Her fingers tingled, her excitement rose.

The speck shifted into a rider.

Anticipation heightened.

Then shriveled. It wasn't her husband.

The horse was a pinto not the big roan Brandon rode. And even from this distance, she'd know her husband with every fiber of her being.

She heaved a deep breath and waited.

As the rider trotted closer, she slid her hand to the worn wooden handle of her 4.75-inch barrel, single-action, six-cylinder Peacemaker.

Jonas did the same.

She frowned. The pinto looked familiar, but it wasn't one of theirs. And instead of a cowboy hat and chaps, the rider wore a sombrero along with a brightly-colored poncho.

Spying her, he yanked the sombrero off his head and waved it.

She recognized the rider and the horse at the same time. Her breath caught then whished out on a mile-wide smile.

"It's okay, Jonas. I know him."

Now sure there was no trouble brewing, he nodded, raised his hand to the approaching rider, and putting heels to his horse's ribs, galloped off.

"Manuel." She jumped off the porch and ran toward the boy who'd went in search of Brandon when she'd holed up at the mission awaiting the birth of the twins.

He leaped off his horse and grabbed her in a bear-hug.

The term boy no longer applied. He was muscled and lean. A man. A young man, but still a man.

"What are you doing here? Is your family well? Sisters Sarah and Marie? Father Jon?" The questions tumbled over each other.

The smile on his face fell away.

Something was wrong. Dreadfully wrong. Stomach knotting, she took a step back and waited, dread seeping through her pores.

"I'm sorry to bring this burden to you. Father Jon and Sister Marie were okay when I left, but Sister Sarah and half the children are sick. Very sick. Two young ones have already succumbed. I didn't know where else to turn. There is no doctor. My mother and sister are helping as best they can."

"What's wrong with them?" Unease crawled up Alex's spine, making her muscles quiver and jump.

He didn't answer immediately.

"Manuel?"

"Smallpox."

"Smallpox?" she whispered. Her pulse stuttered and her limbs turned cold. Smallpox was deadly, especially to children. Most didn't survive. She clenched her fists and closed her eyes. Icy droplets of perspiration popped on her forehead. Not this. Anything but this. Smallpox killed as surely as a bullet to the heart but not as cleanly. She'd do anything for the mission folk but she hated sickness. Sickness that led to death. The smells. The closed in feeling. The helplessness. The inability to save a life. She wasn't cut out to nurse the sick. Fight off rustlers and killers yes. But take care of the sick? She shuddered.

As quickly as the fear and denial hit, it lifted, leaving her shamed. The good sisters and Father Jon had taken her in when she needed them. Had saved not only her life but that of her babies. She straightened her spine. She had a debt to pay and like her husband, she always paid her debts.

"Since you've traveled such a distance, I take it the sickness hasn't affected you?"

"No. My sister and mother made sure I kept my distance from them and the mission. I leave food, supplies and water at the gate. They won't let me come in."

"That's good."

"Do you have a doctor on this great ranch? One that can go back with me? I wouldn't ask, but there's no one else. No doctors in our small village. Father Jon and the good sisters are as close to healers as the village has." Eagerness warred with exhaustion on his smooth young features.

"We have no doctor at Silverhills."

His face fell and despair coated his features.

"I'll go back with you, Manuel."

"Oh no, Senora. This horrible disease is a death's head. You mustn't go." His eyes widened, his expression horrified.

"The good sisters and father saved my life."

He shook his head. "No. It will not do. And I'm sure your husband would not allow it." Relief washed over his features. Manuel had met Brandon on the trail and like most was in awe of him.

"My husband is on a cattle drive. Besides, he doesn't tell me what to do." Not that he didn't try.

Sometimes he succeeded and sometimes he didn't. She was both amused and touched at Manuel's protective male nature.

"You must think of your children."

"I am," she said quietly, as a vise tightened around her heart at the idea of leaving them. Maybe never seeing them again. So much could go wrong. "Sarah Marie and Jon wouldn't be with me today if it hadn't been for the good father and sisters."

"I shouldn't have come," he muttered, twisting his sombrero in his hands.

"Of course, you should have."

His eyes were shadowed and he weaved on his feet.

Instinctively, she reached out an arm then felt his forehead. She breathed a sigh of relief. It was warm, but not dangerously so.

"I'd invite you in, but all things considered it might be better if you aren't around anyone else."

"It's been fourteen days since I've seen anyone and I've kept my distance, but I agree."

"I'll be back with some coffee and breakfast for you."

"Thank you."

Boot heels clicking, she strode into the house.

She returned with a plate of fried bread, steak and eggs, and a steaming cup of coffee. The scents wafted on the warm summer air vying with dust, horses and cattle.

"I'll be back in a few minutes."

He nodded and dropped into one of the two reddish-hued pine rockers that sat on the wide porch.

"This isn't a good idea," he said between woofed down bites, but he was talking to her back.

Fingers thrumming on thighs, she strode through the house and up the stairs.

Two young tornadoes came running toward her on short sturdy legs, followed by Lisa, a babe in her arms, as Alex trotted toward her room.

"Momma. Momma." Two chubby pairs of arms wrapped around her legs. She looked down into emerald eyes so like Brandon's it hurt her heart.

"Jon." She ruffled his hair.

"Momma. Momma."

The little girl had the mischievous smile of her uncle and his sky-blue eyes but her hair was her mother's.

Alexandria scooped them up in her arms and held them close. For a moment, she waivered. What if she didn't make it back? Who would raise her children? Who would love them like she did? Then she snorted. Only every person on the ranch.

"Momma." Sarah pushed away from her mother's too tight grip.

"Sorry, my darlings." Alex loosened her grasp.

Lisa studied her, concern reflected on her delicate features.

"What's wrong?" she mouthed.

"Where's Maria?"

"Right behind you." She tossed her chin in the general direction of Alex's right shoulder.

Alex turned to see a plump woman with honey-colored skin, dark eyes and black hair streaked with silver hurrying toward her.

"Maria, would you take these two for a while?"

Maria nodded and scooped up the twins.

A rush of love swept through Alex. Maria had taken care of her during the torturous days of being enslaved by the Comancheros. And she had taken care of Maria ever since. More like they took care of each other, she amended silently.

Maria arched her eyebrows, mute since the Comancheros cut out her tongue.

Alex shook her head, giving her friend a bright smile that she knew didn't fool her one bit.

"Later," she said softly. Not adding it would probably be several weeks later. She turned to Lisa. "Come with me." Her shoulders twitched as she hurried to her room, Maria's gaze boring into her back.

As soon as Lisa and her nephew were in the bedroom, she closed the door behind her. Her damp palms planted on the polished mahogany wood, her back pressed against it.

"What's wrong?" Lisa asked, worry in her eyes.

Alex pushed away from the door, headed to the large armoire, with entwined leaves carved in an arch across the top, pulled out her carpetbag and began throwing clothes into it.

"Alex?" Apprehension raised Lisa's soft voice an octave.

Seb, her baby, made a fussing noise and began to squirm.

Lisa rocked him back and forth.

Alex paused, a couple of her split-riding skirts,

that Missus Simms made specifically for her, along with her boy's trousers, in her hand.

"You're the only one that will understand why I have to go. Well, possibly Brandon." She sighed. "I hope he will, anyway." She dropped the skirts and trousers into the bag where they landed with a soft thud, then pulled out shirts.

"Go where, Alex?"

"The sisters and Father Jon are in trouble."

"How do you know?"

"Manuel came to get me. Actually, he came for a doctor, but other than Cookie we don't have one and I won't let Cookie go."

"Then you better not tell him where you're headed."

Alex nodded her agreement.

"Where's Manuel? I'd like to see him."

"I'm afraid you can't." And here came the tricky part. She'd hoped to avoid telling anyone about the sickness at the mission. Even with Lisa, who had spent more time at the mission under the sisters' and the father's loving care than Alex had, it was going to be hard for her to accept.

"Why not?"

Alex waited for a moment, marshalling her thoughts, trying to figure out the best way to tell her sister-in-law and friend. Unfortunately, there was no best way so she spilled it bluntly. "Smallpox."

The burgundy duvet rustled as Lisa sank onto it, her expression stricken.

"Oh, Alex, no. You can't go."

"There's no one else, Lisa." She reached over her head to the top shelf of the armoire and threw a couple of boxes of bullets into the bag.

"Who'll take care of the twins?"

"Everyone on the ranch. I'm no longer breastfeeding, remember?" She paused, bag in hand. "There is no one else."

"I'll go," Lisa whispered.

Alex fisted her hands on her hips. Half-amused, half-exasperated.

"Who'll take care of Seb? You are still breastfeeding."

"Maria can give him goats milk. She keeps a couple."

"Your baby is three months old. He needs his momma, not just her breast milk."

Lisa colored.

How any woman could have been used by the Comancheros and maintained a shred of modesty was beyond her. But that was Lisa.

Alex fastened the copper buckles on her worn blue carpetbag.

"Alex, please don't go. Let me. It's my right as much as yours." Lisa clutched Seb as she rocked him against her, tears streaming down her cheeks.

Love welled up in Alex, her body warmed from her toes upward. Besides being modest, Lisa was the most giving, unselfish person she knew.

"Take care of my babies and buy me some time if you can."

"And Brandon?"

The thought of her impatient, virile husband made her pause. Unwanted longing rushed through her and for the hundredth time she wished he was here beside her. But maybe it was for the best. Even though Brandon would understand, she couldn't say with certainty that he wouldn't prevent her from going. Go himself, but maybe keep her from it. He was protective of his own. To the point it was sometimes an annoyance. But since she was the same there wasn't much she could say.

She only smiled and shook her head.

"You're leaving now?"

"I'm stopping by the cookhouse for supplies then I'm heading out."

"Come back safe to us." Her skirt swishing, Lisa stood and gave her a one-armed hug.

Alex returned it. Then grabbed her bag and hurried out. Chin high. Shoulders straight.

Trotting down the stairs, she headed for the door, wanting to get through it before Martha spotted her. She wasn't sneaking out, exactly, but she sure would like to avoid a dustup with their tiny housekeeper and cook. As the bard would say, though she be small, she be mighty. She had to be to keep her husband Cookie in line.

As she hit the entryway door, Mongrel came galloping down the stairs from the twins' room.

She sighed and her heart tightened. She hated leaving the dog almost as much as the twins. Tail slapping, Mongrel bumped against her thighs.

"Stay with the twins." She rubbed the animal's

warm shaggy head.

Mongrel whined.

Alex didn't doubt her dog knew she was leaving him behind. Taking one last look at the winding stairway, the polished floors that reflected her image, and the spotless white walls where a couple of her paintings hung, she let herself out, ignoring the whimpering and scratching at the door.

Manuel sat sopping up the last of his eggs with the fried bread. She tossed her bag, where it landed with a thump at his feet.

"I'll be right back."

She trotted down the lane and headed for the back of the bunkhouse where the cowboys' cookhouse sat, threw open the door and strode in. The scent of cinnamon and hot yeast greeted her. Her stomach growled.

"Ha. I knew you'd show up. You're like a compass where my cinnamon rolls are concerned."

Cookie puffed out his scrawny chest, hitched up the white flour sack wrapped around his skinny waist and pushed a couple of rolls toward her, followed by the butter dish and a knife.

She grabbed one of the warm buns and slathered it with butter then took a bigger bite than was ladylike. She swore she could feel her stomach smile.

"So, what brings you to my kitchen?"

The question effectively killed her momentary euphoria.

She mumbled incoherently around the large mouthful.

"What's that?" He cupped a hand behind his ear.

She swallowed.

"Martha wants to see you."

"When?"

"Now."

"Why?"

"Don't know."

"Fine." He went stomping out.

"She's at your house," she called after him.

She stuffed the rest of the roll into her mouth —she did love Cookie's cinnamon rolls—jumped up, and started throwing food and medical supplies indiscriminately into a couple of flour bags, tied them together and threw them over her shoulder, then filled up the canteen hanging from its hook near the sink.

Hurrying out of the cookhouse, she trotted toward the barn, nearly mowing down Ralph in her haste.

"Mz. Alex," Ralph hollered.

She waved over her head and kept going.

He turned and followed her into the barn and caught up with her as she threw a saddle over Dancer.

"Where you off to, Mz. Alex?"

"Going to check on the herehorns." Lore, she was telling so many whoppers today she was surprised her pants didn't catch fire. Normally, she shot from the hip and damn the consequences, but every man jack on the ranch and a few of the women—she shuddered when she thought of Martha—would be standing in line to try to prevent her from doing what she had to do and she had neither the time nor the inclination to deal with them.

"With a couple of sacks full of supplies?"

She ignored that as she led Dancer out of the stall.

"Saw a young Mexican out in front of the house eating like he hadn't been fed in days."

Again, she didn't answer but swung into the saddle.

"Took me a moment to realize it was Manuel from the mission." He grabbed Dancer's bridle.

The stallion snorted a warning and threw up its head with enough force to jerk the reins from Ralph's hand.

"Wherever you're going give me a moment to saddle up and I'll go with you."

No questions asked. Just blind loyalty. The loyalty that made all the residents of Silverhills family.

She leaned down and said fiercely, "You stay here and take care of my babies." Then tapped her heels to the big black's flanks and sent the stallion charging out of the barn.

"Alex. Wait," Ralph came running after her.

She galloped up to the house, dust flying in fines spurts under Dancer's wide hooves.

"Let's go, Manuel," she yelled as she passed him, not slowing.

His mouth fell open before he snapped it shut, coughing from the fine particles of dirt that floated his way, thumped down his plate and cup, grabbed her bag, threw himself into the saddle and galloped after her.

CHAPTER 2

Crackle. Pop.

Tangerine-colored embers leaped high in an ebony sky. The scent of wood smoke and coffee threaded the dark. Comforting. Reminiscent of cattle drives and camaraderie.

Alex leaned back against a fallen log. Green cotton caught on rough bark. She twitched her shoulders and her shirt pulled free. Looking for a comfortable spot, she shifted as she lifted her tin cup, watching wisps of steam rise as she brought it to her lips.

"Meez Alex."

The timber of Manuel's voice alerted her.

She plopped down the coffee and shot to her feet, her Peacemaker already in her hand. Then she heard it too. The clip-clop of hooves.

"Come out where I can see you with your hands up." Every sense alert, she tried to pierce the dark shadows.

"It's Jeff and Charlie, Alex," Jeff called out as their horses clomped into camp.

Alex let out with every colorful phrase she'd learned from her sailor brother, her husband and the hired hands, finishing with, "What in blazes are you two doing here? You've left the ranch and the people I love unprotected. Dang Ralph anyhow," she finished, having no doubts as to who blabbed to Jeff. Lisa wouldn't have spilled the beans, not even to her beloved husband. At least, not until she was sure Alex had a good head start. With a snap of leather, she holstered her six-gun. Hands fisted on hips, she glared at the two shadowy figures.

The shadows split as Jeff leaped from his horse then pulled his tin cup out of his saddle bag, strode to the fire and poured himself a cup. He grimaced.

"You make the coffee?"

"Don't try to change the subject."

With leather creaking, Charlie swung out of the saddle. Saying nothing, he also poured a cup.

As he sipped, Alex glared at him and said as belligerently as even Cookie could have managed, "You got a complaint about my coffee too?"

Charlie shrugged. "Tastes fine to me."

Her features relaxed fractionally, partially mollified. She turned to Jeff and her frown returned, lines digging into her forehead as her winged eyebrows shot downwards. "Well?"

He gave her a cool look.

"Perhaps, you'd like to explain why you slunk off the ranch, spinning lies and innuendoes, leaving everyone in turmoil and tears."

"I'm sure you exaggerate," she said coolly, though heat shot through her body and inwardly she cringed.

"Am I exaggerating, Charlie?" Jeff asked, his eyes never leaving Alex.

"I make it a point to never get in arguments between the bosses." He sipped his coffee unperturbed.

Alex threw him a grateful look. It was as close to support as she was going to get from anyone.

When she'd first joined Brandon Wade's trail drive, disguised as a boy, Charlie had made her life a living hell. She'd given as good as she'd got and somewhere along the way they'd become fast friends.

"Regardless, I've come to take you back." Jeff took another slug of coffee and grimaced.

Manuel's head bobbed back and forth between the three. At Jeff's statement his features dropped in dismay.

"How do you propose to do that, Jeff?" she asked in a dangerously quiet voice.

"Whatever it takes." He stood tall and hot-eyed, and for a moment reminded her of Brandon. But she couldn't think of her husband now or how much she missed him.

"Planning on shooting me then?"

He rolled his eyes.

"I couldn't outdraw you if I wanted to." He flashed her a grin, anger gone, but plenty of exasperation left.

"And you, Charlie?" She jutted her chin.

"I've got your back, Young Alex," he said quietly, before spitting a wad of tobacco into the flames that caused the fire to jump and sputter.

Both Jeff and Alex stared at him. Jeff's eyebrows jutted up. Alex gave him a look of blinding gratitude.

"Do you know where she's going and why?" Jeff demanded.

"Don't know. Don't care. What I do know is she wouldn't leave her young'uns and the ranch without good reason while her man is gone." He turned to Alex. "Wherever you're going, I'm going with you."

"Oh no, Charlie. I can't let you do that." Her eyes widened, her expression alarmed as cold twisted her innards.

"Don't really see how you can stop me."

"I'll fire you if I have to."

"Do you have any idea how many times I've been fired?" He gave a gravely chuckle and his eyes flashed in amusement.

"Charlie, it's dangerous." She took a step forward and put a hand on his arm.

"I believe I've been insulted." He snorted.

"No. Not that kind of danger." She shook her head vigorously. "There's been an outbreak of smallpox at the mission."

"And you're going?"

"It's different for me. I owe them."

He snorted again.

"If you're going, I'm going." His expression didn't change. He continued to sip his coffee, but there was finality in his voice.

Alex's shoulders slumped, knowing she was beaten.

As one, all eyes turned to Jeff.

Jeff thrummed his fingers on his thighs. After a few heartbeats of silence, he asked, "Have you been inoculated?"

"You know I haven't. The last time Brandon tried

to get the serum in Dodge City, there was none to be had."

"You have young ones at home, Alex. Why are you so hell bent on risking your life?"

"Jeff, I'd have no life and no young ones if it wasn't for the good sisters and father."

He held her gaze then swept a sharp glance at Charlie, who gazed back his face impassive, then at Manuel who was busy studying the tips of his boots. Silence stretched.

Finally, he asked, "Is there anyway I can talk you out of this?"

She shook her head.

He threw up his hands. "Fine. We all go."

"Jeff, I love and appreciate you but you've got to run the ranch. There's no one else. Especially if Charlie is going with me." She threw a glance in the cowhand's direction.

"I'm not going to be the one that tells Brandon I let you go without me." His expressive features betrayed his dilemma. He didn't want to let his sister-in-law ride into danger without his protection nor could he leave the ranch and everything they held dear— especially the children— unprotected.

"Jeff, do you really think Brandon would try to stop me or be able to? He knows what we owe the folks at the mission. You've got to take care of Seb and my babies, and the ranch. Lisa and the rest of the folks are depending on you. And you've got to take care of my herehorns," she added firmly. The new breed of cattle might have been Brandon's brainchild, but she had taken it into her capable hands and ran with it. Now, they were beginning to get recognition and people were buying them to start their own herds.

He grinned at the herehorn comment then sobered and shook his head.

"I'll have her back," Charlie said.

Jeff gave him a long look. "I'm counting on it." Then he turned to Alex. "You win. But I don't like it. Not one little bit and Brandon sure as hell isn't going to."

"No, but he'll understand." Behind her back, she crossed her fingers.

CHAPTER 3

"It's not too late to change your mind, Charlie."

Astride Dancer, Alex watched the rising sun sparkle on Jeff's Arabian's pale flank, before horse and rider disappeared over the rise, leaving only spurts of settling dust.

"Let's go, Young Alex." Charlie turned his chestnut mare and galloped south. Saddles creaking, Manuel and Alex fell in alongside.

On a gray afternoon, six days later, they reined in at the Rio Grande. Blue water tinged with a hint of green lapped at the gritty shore where occasional sage brush and sparse, stringy grass clung to the water's edge.

"This is the lowest point to cross." Manuel pointed at the lapping waves in front of him.

"How deep?" Charlie leaned over and spit a stream of tobacco juice that landed in a nearby bush and dripped to the ground.

"Six maybe eight feet."

"What about there?" Charlie pointed down the river to his left where the channel narrowed, with sandy banks and no bracken. The opposite shore reaching out like a thumb on a closed hand.

"It drops off to over forty feet."

"Your call, Young Alex." Charlie gathered his reins.

She studied the river. A wind had blown up making the waves choppy. The inlet Charlie had pointed to would definitely be quicker. A hard, fast swim for the horses. But if horse or rider lost their balance and went under, they could easily drown. Thinking about going down into all that cold dense wet, as the blue of the river became murky and dark, had fear coating her system. Goosebumps popped on her skin. She took a hard swallow.

"We'll cross here. It'll take longer but the chances of our survival are better."

"Then let's get 'er done." Charlie clucked to his horse. With a snort, the chestnut trotted into the water then began to swim. Hooves slapped against liquid, arcing a fine spray of droplets that hovered momentarily in the air before plunking back into the river.

Dancer snorted and sidled.

"Don't care much for this idea, boy?" She looked at the sky turning gray. Now low and sullen. Then back to the waves that were licking higher and swatting hungrily at the shore. She patted the black's neck, leaned over and whispered, "I don't care much for it either, but as Charlie said, 'let's get 'er done'." She touched boots to flanks and with a snort and a splash, the mighty stallion leaped into the river.

Manuel followed. His black and white pinto's legs churning the frothy water.

It took a moment for Alex to realize that the

droplets splatting her were no longer coming from Dancer's wide hooves. The hovering dark clouds had lowered and opened. The howling wind picked up, causing the waves to rise then fall, slapping against restless currents as they came back down. Beneath her knees, Dancer's sides heaved as the stallion's barrel-chest thrust against a river that was fast turning on them.

The horses pushed on, sinew and muscle bunching and stretching, swimming strongly.

They were halfway across when disaster struck.

CHAPTER 4

The wind bit. The crystal-colored, sharp-as-shards spray stung as it hit Alex in the face. Under her, Dancer's powerful legs churned, the bank on the other side hard to see through the rain. They could be close. They could be a mile away.

Ahead of her, Charlie's valiant mare pushed through the weighted water. Rain pouring off the brim of his hat, Charlie glanced over his shoulder. She raised her hand. He did the same, then turned back in his saddle, focusing his attention on his horse.

Alex took a quick look at Manuel.

Horror filled her.

As she watched, the pounding elements whipped the waves and hit the pinto head on, pushing at the horse's eyes and filling its nostrils. For a moment, the stallion shook its head and stopped swimming. And in that brief second, went under.

"Manuel!" Her breath caught. The wind and rain hit the back of her throat and choked her, whipping her words away.

A moment later, the horse fought its way upward. First, its head visible then its body, but there was no rider. The horse began to swim strongly in her direction.

"Manuel," she screamed above the winds. She squinted, swiping the rain and river out of her eyes. Nothing.

She wiped her eyes again.

There! Manuel's head bobbed up, his hat riding on his shoulders, the rawhide tie under his chin digging into his throat. He went down then surfaced again. His multi-colored serape lay on the water like a soggy blanket. Slowly it sank into the Rio, pulling Manuel with it.

He fought his way back up just as the current changed, dragging him down the middle of the river.

Without thought, she dove off Dancer. The horse screamed as she left the saddle. Muscles taut, arms stretching, she swam toward Manuel. The current carrying her. Gray waves, at times higher than her head, washed over her. Her heart pounding, she closed her eyes, breathed as best she could and went with the current.

"Meez Alex."

Blinking rapidly, she floated on top of the swells. Squinting, legs paddling, she rotated around, searching for a glimpse of her friend.

"Manuel." There he was! Only half a dozen feet from her, trying to fight his way toward her.

Something was wrong. He was only using one arm.

Again, she let the current carry her. He continued to push his way toward her, swimming with his right arm. She'd almost reached him when a swell covered him and he disappeared.

"Manuel," she yelled above the roar of the river. She splashed in a frantic circle, but could see nothing but water.

"Meez Alex." The voice carried faintly above the roar. Again, she circled.

There! Arms reaching, legs kicking, she swam in his direction.

"Go back, Meez Alex. I'll follow." He no sooner said it then a wave carried him under.

"Manuel. Manuel." Her heartbeat, already rapid, sped up. Where was he? He should have surfaced by now.

She fought her way toward where she'd last seen him. Something bumped against her leg and she hauled him to the surface. He coughed out water and gasped for air.

"Let me go. The current is too strong."

Instead of heeding him, she grabbed the neck of his serape and began to swim with one hand. He did the same. The river fought her. Pushed against her. Her burning lungs pumped hard. Her arms and legs leaden.

Her strokes slowed.

Whoosh.

Something slapped her on the shoulder. Stinging.

Charlie's lasso lay on the water. She reached for it. Missed.

Then grabbed again. She could almost touch it with her fingertips. A wave splashed, carrying it away.

Charlie drew it back in and again let it fly. It

splashed nearby. She reached out, her muscles stretching, her fingers spread and searching. This time she snagged it. He nodded and nudged his horse forward. She hung on as he dragged them through the water. The progress slow, their weight holding back Charlie's horse.

Suddenly, a black shape loomed through the wet and the dark. Followed by a trumpet of sound.

"Dancer." The stallion was close enough she could feel the damp heat coming off the horse's powerful body. Relief slicked her already soaked skin.

"Here, Manuel. Take the rope and let Charlie haul you." She tossed him the rope then grabbed a stirrup and fought her way into the saddle. Mighty hooves churning the water, Dancer swam forward, Alex hanging onto the pommel, making no attempt to grab the reins and guide the horse. Dancer would get them to shore. Behind them, Manuel held onto the rope with one hand as Charlie towed him in.

Welcome as a miracle, Dancer's gait changed. The stallion was no longer swimming but galloping, hooves sinking into wet grit that popped and squelched. They'd made it to the shallows.

Her arms drooped around the stallion's wet, slick neck. A few more yards. She just had to hang on for a moment or two longer.

The gallop dropped to a squishy plod before the big horse halted altogether, head lowered, blowing.

She tumbled out of the saddle, resting her head against the sleek, damp neck.

"You saved me. Again."

Few understood the connection between Alex and the stallion, but the ranch hands had seen the horse come charging to her rescue too many times to question it.

A sucking sound came from her right. She looked up to see Charlie's valiant mare hit the damp ground. On shaky legs, she hurried forward to help haul her young friend in. They let go of the rope as he reached the shallows and staggered to his feet.

Charlie went after Manuel's horse who stood trembling a few feet away.

"Thanks, Meez Alex," Manuel gasped out.

She nodded then dropped to the ground, her breath raspy.

With a creak of wet leather, Charlie climbed out of his saddle, pulled out his pocket watch, then shook his head in disgust as water gushed out of it. Next, he blinked up into the rain that seemed to be lessening as he searched the sky for a sun that refused to show its face.

"I'm thinking it's late afternoon. Let's find a place to take shelter and call it a day."

Alex stood. Her legs shaking so badly she could barely stay on her feet. She glanced at Manuel who looked in worse shape than she. Then lastly at the exhausted horses, Dancer's nostrils flared and red. As much as she wanted to push on, Charlie was right.

"Good plan," she said. "Now where do we find shelter?"

"If we backtrack along this side of the river about a quarter of a mile, there's a small cave we could shelter in," Manuel said. The words coming out on a wheeze, his wet chest rising and falling.

"I noticed you were favoring your arm. How is it?" Alex asked.

"It's nothing. I knocked it against a log in the water. Just bruised." To prove it, he moved it up and down. Biting his lip and trying not to grimace.

"Let me see," Alex said.

"It's nothing," Manuel repeated.

She pushed up his sleeve. His upper arm was red and swollen, but no bones protruded.

"It's gonna be sore, but nothing's broken." Relief coated her voice.

"I'm fine." He pulled back his arm and rolled down his sleeve.

"Let's get moving then," Charlie said.

They mounted and headed back to where they'd planned to cross, before being swept upstream, and headed inland.

The rain turned to drizzle. The horses plodded on. Water drops plopped off brims of hats. Exhausted, Alex swayed in the saddle lulled by the sounds of squelching hooves. Her eyes drooped.

A rabbit streaked in front of the horses. Dancer shied in one direction, the pinto and chestnut in the other. Alex slid abruptly to the right, then grabbed the saddle pommel as she started to fall and hauled herself back up.

The black stallion came to an abrupt halt, turned his head around and shook it.

"All right. All right," she grumbled. "I'll pay more

attention."

Charlie, his mount now settled, looked at her and grinned. "I swear you and that hoss have a language of your own."

"Lucky for me, he can't talk."

Dancer threw his head up and down, and snorted.

Manuel's eyes widened and his mouth dropped.

"Just coincidence, son." Charlie chortled.

Manuel didn't look convinced but nodded.

"How much farther?" Charlie asked.

Manuel pointed.

Ahead lay a ridge with an overhang closer to the bottom than the top. The grey of the stone blending with the sullen sky. The black yawning hole of a cave beneath it.

The tightness between Alex's shoulder blades lessened and her shoulders slumped. She had an overwhelming desire to weep and she never cried. Instead, she straightened in the saddle. "Let's go."

In less time than expected, they were under the overhang and out of the wet. The ground and everything on it damp. But at least there was no water dripping from their hats and plopping on their shoulders. She turned to Dancer, threw up the stirrup, unbelted the cinch, and reached for her saddle. Before she could grab it, Charlie plucked it up and walked into the cave.

"I could have gotten that, but I thank you." She followed him in.

"Why don't you sit down, Young Alex."

She removed the bridle then plopped down on the cool damp ground and leaned against her wet saddle.

"Do you want me to hobble him?" Manuel asked, his expression leery.

"No need."

Manuel started to cross himself then saw both of them watching him and stopped.

"It's nothing magical, Manuel. He just doesn't stray far from me. I never hobble him."

Manuel gave her a shamefaced look. "I guess I was too tired to pay any attention past taking care of my own horse."

"Why don't you gather whatever might be in the cave in the way of twigs, leaves and bones," Charlie suggested.

"I'll help." Just the thought made her body ache. But fair was fair. She started to push to her feet.

"How 'bout if you take care of the fire and coffee tomorrow morning, and Manuel and I will sleep in."

"That's—" Her voice caught in her throat, her heart thundered and her hands shook as she strained to hear. Afraid she'd hear, what she'd heard a moment before. It came again.

Rattle. Rattle.

Without moving her head, she rolled her eyes to the side.

Even coiled up, it was a dang big snake, with a mean look in its flat eyes. Its head up, its tail rattling.

Beads of ice-cold sweat popped on her brow. It was all she could do to stop the violent trembling that tried to steal over her body. She knew if it started her entire bones would shake. She gritted her teeth and locked them.

Charlie was still talking but it came as a low buzz in the background. She prided herself on her courage, but she was deathly afraid of snakes.

She closed her eyes and tried to regulate her breathing.

Before she could wheeze out a breath, a sound like thunder roared through the cave, bouncing and echoing off the walls. The snake jumped forward in two parts. She leaped out of the way burying her head in her arms. The scent of sulfur and blood filled the confined area. Cautiously, she lifted her head. She watched Charlie holster his gun.

"I hate snakes," she muttered.

"I remember." He grinned.

Her bones loosened and she grinned back. When she'd first joined the cattle drive, masquerading as a boy, Charlie had placed a garter snake in her boot. In return, she'd placed a small amount of May apple root in his stew. Not enough to kill him, but enough to make him sick. After trying to throttle each other, they'd become friends.

Charlie picked up the two halves of the snake and Alex inched herself and her saddle away from the remaining pieces of skin, meat and blood.

Manuel built a fire that hissed and smoked. In spite of the poor quality of the flames, her damp cloths warmed and began to dry.

Her head drooped as she listened to the drip-drip of raindrops on soil and stone. In moments, lulled by the rain, she slept.

She awoke at dawn to the rumble of thunder, hard

pellets of liquid splatting against earth, and something else. A low humming and quiver of stone. She leaped to her feet and looked wildly around.

Outdoors, wet dripping off his slicker and hat, Charlie strode toward the cave. He reached the lip as a rumbling sounded and rock and mud spewed from the top of the ledge.

"Charlie, look out!" She raced forward. Ice slicked her veins and a silent scream lodged in her throat as a small boulder knocked the cowboy to the ground.

CHAPTER 5

Horses snorted. Cattle lowed. Lariats slapped against chaps.

Pockets of dust rose beneath Herefords' and horses' hooves. A small group of men flipped their lassos and yipped, driving half a dozen curly red cattle up an incline dotted with sagebrush and wild grass where a lone rider stared down at a sprawling ranch in the valley below.

Leather creaked as Brandon Wade leaned against the saddle pommel to study the ranch. Somber brown-toned wood buildings, trimmed with grey stone, contrasted sharply with the lush green of grass and bushes, and the occasional colorful wildflower, that surrounded them.

Silverhills. Home.

Over the past months, he'd longed for his children and ached for his wife. The trail drives were necessary but the time away got harder and harder.

He'd had the Herefords shipped from back East to Dodge. The cattle would strengthen their herd of herehorns, a blend of Hereford and longhorn beef. A gift of sorts for O'Malley. Something she'd appreciate more than jewelry or fancy perfume.

As he watched, Sam the blacksmith led a frisky bay down the road. Even from here Brandon could see the bulge of arm muscles that spent most days hammering horseshoes. George, who lived next to Sam, was chasing a piglet that had escaped the confines of his pen, running in the opposite direction. And Missus Simms, the seamstress, hurried toward the main house, a calico dress slung over her arm.

Silverhills was more village than ranch. It only lacked a doctor to be completely self-sufficient. His father had built it and Brandon had expanded it. Strengthened it. Smoothed the rough edges.

He was at school out East when his parents were killed. He'd come home and picked up the reins. Running the ranch. Watching over his baby brother. And never looking back. A successful ranch to begin with, he'd turned it into a thriving community.

He'd never realized anything was missing in his life until Alexandria O'Malley came barreling into it. Now everything centered around her. He'd give up the ranch in a minute if it meant keeping or saving his wife. Not that it would ever come to that, he thought ruefully, she loved Silverhills and its people as much as he did. If possible, more.

The need to see her as strong as the need to breathe, he nudged Eagle, his roan, forward. Horse and rider surged down the hill, an eager smile on Brandon's rugged features, his pulse racing in time with the fast thump of his roan's mighty hooves.

His eager gaze on the ranch, he didn't notice the oversized jack rabbit until it darted under his horse's nose before disappearing into the underbrush.

Eagle shied hard to the right.

Brandon slipped, his hind end in the air instead of the saddle, where it hung for several breathless seconds. Then horse and rider regained their balance and Eagle galloped on. He cursed the rabbit then forgot it. Silverhills his lodestar.

As he neared the house, he loped past a cowhand, acknowledging the man with a jerk of his chin. He brought Eagle to a stiff-legged halt in front of the house, leaped from the saddle, looped the reins, and slapped his horse on the rump. With a toss of its sleek head, Eagle trotted toward the stables, where oats and hay waited. Ralph came out of the stable as the horse reached it. He looked around, saw Brandon, and raised his hand in acknowledgement before leading the stallion into the large wooden structure.

Heels clicking on wood, Brandon trotted up the veranda steps, threw open the door and bellowed, "O'Malley."

The first person that came hurrying from the bowels of the house was Martha, Cookie's wife, diminutive in stature, but a force to be reckoned with, wiping her hands on the white apron wrapped around her waist.

"Thank goodness you're home."

The first trickle of unease crept through him, making his shoulders twitch. Martha had been at Silverhills since he was a young'un and her not much older. Now she was the housekeeper-cook of the ranch house and ran the place with an efficiency that would do a drill sergeant proud. Normally unflappable, worry sparked her eyes.

"What's wrong?"

Before she could answer, small feet came clattering across the floor.

"Poppa. Poppa." Squeals of delight had him grinning. He squatted down and scooped up his children. Jon who looked just like his daddy. And Sarah Marie, who except for her uncle's blue eyes, was a miniature of her mother, right down to her independent spirit and fiery temper, and had him wrapped around her finger because of it.

"Momma?" Sarah Marie asked.

"Momma?" Jon parroted.

His jaw clenched along with his heart. His grip on his children tightened, causing them both to squirm. Sarah Marie demanding, "Down."

He put them on the ground and straightened to look straight into the eyes of the mute Maria who had been hard on their heels. Maria, who'd had her tongue cut out by the Comancheros and had befriended Alex when she'd been captured. And what he read on her expressive round features made his blood run cold.

CHAPTER 6

"What happened?" The words were forced out of jaws that had a tendency to lock.

Maria whipped out the notebook and pencil she always carried in the pockets of her skirts. Before she could write anything, Martha spoke out, agitation in her voice, fire in her eyes, "I would have stopped her if I'd had the least idea what she was about," adding, "somehow."

Impatience mounted.

The door swung open and slammed shut as Cookie came stomping in, flour specks on his blue shirt.

The pressure in Brandon's head built till he thought it might blow straight off. He shoved the words through gritted teeth, "Will someone please explain what is going on and tell me where in hell my wife is?"

As Martha and Cookie drew breath to explain, Maria who'd been scratching on her tablet, held it up.

She's on her way to Mexico.'

His breath whished out and his knees tried to sag.

By now Martha and Cookie were both talking, each raising their voice, trying to drown the other out.

He figured Cookie would be briefer and more succinct. He was wrong. He held up a finger. Cookie hushed, grumbling under his breath.

He turned to Martha. "Why is my wife in Mexico?"

"That young Mexican came and got her."

"What young Mexican?"

"You know the one."

By this time, he was ready to stomp on his hat and howl.

Once again Maria held up her notebook.

'From the mission.'

"Manuel?"

Maria nodded vigorously.

His heart clenched. Something was wrong at the mission or Manuel would never have come.

Sarah Marie went toddling toward the kitchen. Maria gave him a wide-eyed plea to help her friend then went after the toddler.

Martha scooped up Jon and once again both she and her husband began talking at once.

"Brandon. Thank goodness you're home." Steps sounded from the gallery and Lisa came hurrying down the stairs.

His boot heels clicked in a sharp tattoo as he trotted up the stairs, meeting her halfway.

"Lisa. What in thunder is going on?"

She took a deep breath. There were new worry lines around her mouth and her smooth textured skin strained tight across bones, but she carried her chin high and her eyes held his, steady.

"She's gone to the mission."

"Why?"

"They have an outbreak of smallpox."

A chill coursed through him and his throat went dry.

"The children are sick. Some have already died." Distress flashed in normally clear, cornflower-blue eyes now sunken and dark.

The blood drained from his head and the vise around it tightened. *Smallpox.* And his wife was throwing herself headfirst into the deadly contagion. She wasn't inoculated. None of them were. It wasn't that easy to get the vaccine out West, especially on a ranch with no towns nearby.

His hands formed fists and tightened till scarred knuckles turned white.

She picked one up in both of hers. "I hate it and I'm scared to death, but she had to go. You know that." Distress and defeat entered her voice. "I would have gone with her if she'd have let me."

He was too distracted to state the obvious. She couldn't have left Seb.

Fear and fury filled him. How dare Alexandria put her life in harm's way. She wasn't just responsible for herself. She had the twins to think of...and him.

Lisa looked like she'd like to turn and run from what she saw in his face. Instead, she shifted a hand to his arm and repeated, "She had to go. She couldn't have lived with herself if she hadn't. She's just not made that way. You know how much she loves you and the twins. She'd never willingly leave any of you. You're her life."

His shoulders slumped. Fury drained. Lisa was

right. He wouldn't love her if she was anything less than what she was. High-hearted and mule-stubborn. The two things that could get her killed. He fought against the despair washing through him. He turned to head back down the stairs.

"She's not alone."

He spun around, his heel meeting air, but he managed to right himself. "You mean Manuel?"

"I mean Charlie."

"Charlie? I'm surprised she let him accompany her."

"She didn't." For the first time Lisa grinned.

"Oh, she didn't?" Brandon's eyebrows shot up.

"She hightailed it out of here before anyone could stop her. Charlie and Jeff went after her, and Jeff came back alone. She insisted Jeff come back to take care of the ranch, me and the young ones. She said the same to Charlie, but he didn't budge."

She grinned again.

His heart lightened and he grinned back. There wasn't a man jack on the ranch that wouldn't lay down their life for her, figuring she felt pretty much the same about them. And, because she was his.

"Thank you."

"Are you heading out?"

"Yes."

"Godspeed. Bring my friend back."

"I intend to." He went galloping down the stairs, gleaming with so much shine he could see his grim reflection in them. Maria and Martha stood at the bottom of the staircase, waiting for him. Cookie gone.

"Stop by the cookhouse and have Cookie gather you up some supplies," Martha said as he threw open the door.

He nodded and headed for the stable, where he quickly resaddled Eagle and led the horse out.

As he threw himself in the saddle a voice rang out, "Hold up there."

Striding toward him with his rolling, bull-legged gait came Cookie, two flour sacks thrown over his shoulders. He tossed them up to Brandon. "Bring that dang, hard-headed girl home," he commanded.

"Count on it." He wheeled his horse and galloped out of the ranch. A cloud of dust in his wake.

CHAPTER 7

Thunder roared. Lightning speared. The earth trembled.

"Charlie!" she screamed as the storm's fury slicked soil and loosened rocks, sending them pinging and tumbling around the cave's entrance.

Gray shale stung Alex's face and shoulders as she and Manuel raced out of the cave. The small boulder, that bounced off Charlie, tumbled to a stop, wet as the leaden sky. Dark as the cave's interior.

Holding his arm, Charlie pushed to his feet.

"Are you alright?"

He winced as she ran her fingers up and down the arm he held.

"What's wrong?"

"Dislocated shoulder. I heard it pop." He looked her in the eye. "You're going to have to push it back in."

Her stomach heaved. She swallowed bile that rose to the back of her throat, bitter and hot, straightened her shoulders and gave a sharp tip of her chin in acknowledgement. "I'm assuming you've got whiskey in your saddle bag."

"It's a little earlier than I normally start but yeah I do," he joked, giving her a weak smile.

"Manuel, would you get the bottle out of his saddle bag?" she called over her shoulder, her gaze never leaving Charlie's.

"Si, Senora." The young man hurried to the corner of the cave where Charlie's gear sat, shoved up against the cool wall of stone. The bottle clicked against Charlie's spare Colt Patterson Revolver, as Manuel pulled it out of a worn saddlebag. He trotted back and handed it to Charlie.

The cowhand took a swig then passed the bottle to Alex.

"I believe I will." She took a deep swallow and came up coughing as her belly heated, then wiped her mouth, stoppered the bottle and handed it back to Manuel.

"Build a fire and get the coffee going, will you, Manuel?"

He nodded and began scrounging the cave for leaves, limbs and bones.

"Sit down and hold your arm away from your body."

Charlie slid down the cave wall to the rock and grit of the floor's surface.

Alex squatted down and grabbed his good shoulder to hold him in place. No heat radiated through the gray, dusty cotton of his shirt. His body cold to the touch.

With her other hand, keeping his elbow bent, she gently pulled his injured arm toward her.

Her hand trembled. She gulped in air then let it out.

His face white beneath its tan, he grimaced and said between gritted teeth, "Get 'er done."

She nodded, bit her lips together and gave a short, sharp yank.

Click. The bone slid back into the socket.

She lowered his arm then dropped her head into her hands.

Manuel shoved the bottle back at Charlie who took a couple of gulps, his Adam's apple dancing, then passed it to Alex. She took a swallow, coughed again, and again heat flared in her belly.

Charlie gave her a nod.

"Well, I don't have a petticoat to tear up for ya, but I do have an extra blouse I can use," she joked weakly.

"Take my spare shirt. I was planning on buying a new one anyway."

While they joked and argued about it, Manuel came back with one of his own shirts torn into strips.

"Thank you, Manuel."

"Thankee."

"By the way, how is your arm?" Alex took the red, light-weight cotton and wrapped Charlie's shoulder in a sling.

"Better. Much better." Manuel passed out tins of coffee and hardtack.

Alex knew he would have said that regardless, but she let it go.

"You know, Charlie, you can always head back. Manuel and I will be fine," Alex said around a mouthful of the hard, flat bread with a taste of salt to it.

"Young Alex, that's one of the most insulting

things you've ever said to me." Charlie sat down his cup and gave her a steady look.

"Do what you need to do." She fought back the heat that rose in her cheeks. She would have been every bit as insulted if she'd been injured. Nothing short of knocking at death's door would turn her from where she felt her duty lay.

Charlie was the same, and misguided enough to think it lay with her. It warmed her. This sense of family and unity she felt for these tough-minded cow-punchers.

"I don't know what I'd do without you, Charlie."

"You shouldn't have had that second swallower of whiskey, Young Alex."

Still, she could tell he was pleased. He thumped down his tin cup and pushed to his feet. "Daylight's a wasting."

Heaving a sigh, Alex hoisted herself up. It would do no good to try to get him to rest for a bit. Charlie was as stubborn as a mule. She fought back the urge to help him mount, knowing it wouldn't be appreciated. Nor later during the day when she suggested they take a short break was that appreciated either.

Shamed relief washed through her. Not that she wasn't worried about Charlie, but the thought of smallpox running ruthlessly through the mission scared her spitless as she fretted for the inhabitants. Willow bark traveled in one of the flour sacks tied across Dancer's haunches. It was the only thing she knew to treat the fever and the pain. Somehow, she would get her friends and the children through this.

She would save them just as they had saved her. Shoulders thrust back, chin jutting at a determined angle, she turned her attention to the trail.

As the day progressed they climbed higher, the air in the mountains thinning as the occasional loosened rock went tumbling down the mountainside underneath large hooves.

The rain had stopped, but the sky still roiled with grey, when she heard a scream that sent shivers down her spine.

Puma! She twisted in the saddle and looked around. Nothing. Probably hidden in the timber. Dancer snorted and tossed his head. Apparently, not liking the hair-raising sound any more than she did.

The scream came again. Piercing. Nearly human. Causing goosebumps to roughen her skin.

And again. Filled with anger, pain and terror.

Alex left the trail they'd been following and wound her way into the brush and up the mountain.

"Where's she going?" she heard Manuel ask.

"Alex, don't," Charlie called, cursing as he turned his horse to follow her.

"That cat is in pain, Charlie."

"That's when they're the most dangerous."

She urged Dancer up the steep incline, pebbles and dirt upended as powerful legs bunched and jumped.

"I haven't a hope in hades of you listening to me. Might as well tell the wind not to blow," he grumbled.

Large hooves crushed occasional scrub grass and loosened a fine coating of dirt as the horses climbed. The roar of the cat increased in volume. Charlie continued to mutter. Manuel said nothing, just followed the other two.

They rounded a curve and saw the cat. Female and magnificent.

Reddish-brown fur, amber eyes and looked to weigh a hundred pounds. The puma lay in front of a cave. One leg weighed down by rocks from a cave-in, snarling a warning.

First Charlie and now the cat. The wind, thunder, lightning and torrential rains must have cut a swath across the path they traveled, she thought.

"Whatever you're planning. You better hope she doesn't have kits in that cave or you'll never get to her without being torn apart." Charlie jerked Alex out of her preoccupation of the weather.

"From the looks of her belly, I'd say she's carrying the kits, but hasn't birthed them yet."

"You may be right." Charlie studied the cat's protruding belly. "The kindest thing would be to shoot her and put her out of her misery."

Was it? It would certainly put her out of her pain, but what if they killed her when they could have saved her? "How about we get her out from under those rocks and then make that decision?"

"And how do you propose to do that?" Charlie asked with commendable calm.

"Meez Alex, you aren't going to try to free that cat, are you?" Manuel's young voice had risen an octave.

"Now, Manuel, you really don't think Young Alex would do anything that hairbrained, do you?"

For a moment, relief flashed across Manuel's features then was dashed when Alex responded.

"Is that sarcasm I hear, Charlie?"

The cat snarled. The horses stomped and snorted, sidling nervously.

"What's your plan?" Resignation writ on Charlie's leathery features.

"I'm going to try to loosen the rocks around the edges of the entrance and hopefully the ones holding her leg will roll away." She gave a hard swallow and her stomach flopped.

"I'll do it." Charlie yanked off his sling and started to dismount.

"Wait."

He settled back into the saddle. "Changed your mind?" he asked without much hope.

"You're injured and you aren't as fast as I am, if there's a need to run."

"If?"

"Okay, when there's a need to run."

"You may be able to move the smaller ones, but you ain't budging that largish one."

"If I can move the smaller rocks on top of it, we can lasso it and pull it off."

"Then run."

"Then run." She laughed.

"Get 'er done." He drew his gun.

She lifted an eyebrow.

"If it comes to you or the cat, I choose you. And me for that matter. If this gets back to Brandon, he will skin me alive. And that's no exaggeration."

"It will be our secret," she assured him, not wanting Brandon to get wind of this any more than Charlie.

She leaped off Dancer and began moving rocks that were out of range of the cat's sharp claws and teeth.

The cat continued to snarl and try to leap at Alex as she pulled the rocks away around the edge of the cave, hoping the large stones holding the cat in place would tumble aside.

Rocks toppled as Alex pulled and threw them, soon covered in dust and sweat.

"You're going to have to move that large one. It's the king pin. You move that, the rocks holding the cat will fall away."

Her breasts heaving, her breath coming in hard pants, she looked at the large, craggy gray rock and the smaller ones surrounding the puma.

"You're right." She strode to Dancer and pulled her lariat from her saddle horn, strode back and began to wrap the rope around the boulder.

"Look out," Charlie shouted.

As the puma's paw shot out, she did a nimble leap back.

Dancer trumpeted his displeasure. Rising on hind legs, front legs lashing air, the stallion challenged the big cat.

Ears flat, the puma hissed then subsided.

Alex fastened the knot and, as the big horse came down, leaped into the saddle. She backed Dancer up. Tail swishing, hind quarters dancing, the stallion pranced backward, the boulder moving inch by inch, till the rocks surrounding the cat tumbled loose.

"Drop that lasso and let's ride," Charlie bellowed.

"Go, Manuel," Alex called, tossing the rope and wheeling Dancer.

Manuel turned the pinto. Hooves thundering, his horse galloped away. The young man riding low in the saddle, clinging like a burr.

"Go, Young Alex," Charlie yelled.

Now wasn't the time to argue. She touched heels to Dancer's wide flanks. The stallion needed no urging and took off at a run, out pacing the pinto in mere moments and taking the lead.

Alex turned to make sure Charlie was coming and got a branch to the side of her head for her efforts, nearly knocking her from the saddle.

"Go, go, go, go," Charlie yelled as his horse kicked up dust. He and Manuel charging behind her.

She pulled on the reins and motioned Manuel to pass her. As the pinto flew by, she called to Charie, "Is the cat after us?" She trusted the cat had leaped in the opposite direction the moment it was free, but considering the puma was pregnant, hurting and mad, she wasn't hanging her hat on it.

"Not that I can see, but let's not take any chances on being lunch for that animal, okay?"

They charged downhill for another five minutes. The horses slipping and sliding till finally, Alex reined in and looked around. Giddy relief flooded her system. "I think we're in the clear."

Charlie reined in beside her, shaking his head. "Of all the crazy harebrained ideas you've ever had and that includes painting the longhorns' horns red, this was the craziest."

"Come on, Charlie, that turned out to be an excellent idea."

"Mayhap, but don't expect me to say the same about this one."

"If you don't say anything at all, I'll be perfectly happy. Did you get a look at her before we took off?"

"Besides her big pearly whites?"

"Did she look like she would make it?"

"Her paw was pretty bloody and she was limping, but she's got a fifty-fifty shot now thanks to you."

"Thanks to us."

He grunted.

She studied the sky, surprised to see the clouds had dissipated and the sun was sinking, turning the sky purple and red, haloing her surroundings.

"What say we make camp?"

"Yeah, preferably where's there's no mountain cats."

CHAPTER 8

Night tumbled in. Dense as pistol smoke and twice as quiet.

Brandon reined in Eagle. As much as he wanted to push on, he couldn't risk the horse stepping in an unseen hole and breaking a leg. Groaning, he swung out of the saddle, every muscle crying in protest. Except for the brief stop at the ranch, where he discovered his wife was on her way to Mexico, he'd been in the saddle over twelve straight hours. He must be getting old. There was a time he could have ridden all day and night and not felt it.

He unsaddled and rubbed down Eagle, then built a fire, made coffee and dug hardtack out of the sack Cookie had thrust at him. The old rapscallion had also provided a bottle of whiskey for which Brandon was profoundly grateful. He unstopped it and added a dollop to his coffee.

Tossing his saddle up against a log, he lowered himself to the ground and leaned against it. Trail dust coated his clothes, sticky from heat. As he raised his cup, steam from the coffee danced up his nose. The earthy brew warmed his throat. The whiskey his belly.

The nerves crawling under his skin slowed, and

for the first time since he'd gotten the news that his wife had once more put herself in danger, he threw his head back and came as close to relaxing as he was gonna get.

Eagle gave a nervous whicker. Leaves and twigs cracked under huge hooves as the horse shuffled about.

The moment of peace disappeared as quickly as it came.

In one fluid motion, Brandon was on his feet, gun drawn. A few moments later he heard what his horse had, the clomp of hooves and the low voices of approaching riders. Tall trees at his back, he melted into the shadows.

Two men rode in. One big and burly. One thin and young, his eyes shifting about constantly. Firelight shown eerily on their faces, turning them orange, adding a rough and hungry look to their features.

"Hello in camp," the big one called out.

Brandon remained silent. Eagle stilled.

The stranger started to swing out of his saddle.

Brandon stepped out of the trees. "That's far enough."

The hombre looked at the Colt in Brandon's hand and eased back into his saddle.

"Your coffee smells mighty good. How about sharing a cup?"

"It's all gone."

"You could always make some more."

"I could. But I'm not."

"Now, mister, that ain't friendly." The man's tone

changed. His voice hardened. His back straightened.

"I'm not looking to make friends."

The one with the shifty eyes, gave a feral smile. His hand dropped to his gun.

"I wouldn't." Brandon cocked his hammer and aimed his Peacemaker at Shifty Eyes.

"You're making a big mistake," said the bigger man.

"I've made 'em before."

"There's two of us and only one of you." The big man's eyes narrowed, watching him carefully.

"Then that means there's a fifty percent chance, one of you will survive."

"You seem to think a lot of yourself, mister," the big man said.

"My gun is drawn and I never miss."

"Come on, Earl, we can take him," the scrawny one said, his eyes hot, his expression eager.

Brandon pointed the gun at Earl's heart. "What's it going to be, Earl? Your partner may survive. You won't."

One heartbeat. Two. The two men stared at each other with deadly intent. Tension mounted.

"We can take him," Shifty Eyes repeated, his gun hand twitching.

"Leave your gun in your holster. I ain't looking to die tonight," Earl snarled at his partner, his gaze still locked with Brandon's.

Muttering, Shifty Eyes dropped his hand.

Finally, Earl's gaze shifted. "Another time." There was promise in the words. They'd meet again and finish this.

"I look forward to it." And there was promise in those words too.

Earl spit a wad of tobacco into the fire, causing it to hiss and jump in a colorful hue, then turned his horse. The two men rode out of camp.

Only after the clomp of hooves disappeared did Brandon lower his gun. Over the years he'd learned to size up men and those two were as wrong as they came.

Gazing around the camp, he holstered his gun, wondering if he should find a different campsite in case they came back.

He kicked a short, gnarly branch aside. He was too damn tired to break camp and move. Scooping up twigs and brushwood, he laid them around the perimeter of the camp so if the two hombres came back he'd know it and be ready for them, then slumped on his saddle, rolled into his blanket, and fell into an uneasy sleep.

~*~

The lightening of an overcast sky, still sullen and gray, and the chirp of a couple of sparrows—way to cheerful to his way of thinking—woke him.

He rekindled his campfire. Reheated the coffee. Gulped down hardtack and jerky, then threw the remains from the coffeepot onto the fire, causing tangerine-colored embers to hiss, sputter and die.

Climbing into the saddle, he pushed on.

Burning off the heavy mist, the sun beat down,

brutal in its intensity. Brandon reined in, took off his hat and wiped the beads of sweat from his forehead, then shoved his hat back on. He narrowed his eyes and studied the craggy, dust-colored arroyo ahead. If he circled around it, it would cost him an extra day of hard riding.

On the other hand, if the two hombres that he ran off last night were waiting for him, this would be the place. He didn't care for either option. But there was no choice really, not with O'Malley trekking across Mexico where Comancheros and killers holed up in the mountainous terrain.

He straightened in the saddle, gaze alert, tracking the ridges and gullies, then tapped heels to Eagle and moved forward. All he had to do was get through this arroyo then hopefully with another day or two of hard riding, he'd reach the Rio Grande, where somewhere, somehow, he'd find his wife on the other side.

Eagle's hooves clicked against water-scarred shale as the stallion trotted through the high-ridged arroyo. The gully wide enough for two horses to ride side by side but not more. He scanned his surroundings. The best place for an ambush was up ahead on the right. Plenty of cover and still give a good view of below. If he was going to take someone by surprise, that would be the place he'd pick.

He reined the big roan as close to the right of the gully as he could get. The horse snorted as it looked for footing. Brandon's leg brushed the wall, scraping his tanned cowhide chaps and the side of his stirrup. He paid no mind. All his attention focused up ahead, giving Eagle his head, just guiding the horse back if it tried to veer from the path Brandon had chosen.

Nothing moved except a hawk that glided overhead, giving a shrieking call that carried on the hot breeze blowing in Brandon's face.

They plodded forward, getting closer and closer to the high-ridged overhang. Maybe he'd got it wrong. Maybe the two men had cut their losses and rode out. Or maybe they'd found a different spot to ambush him. But his gut told him it was here. Senses alert, he kept his gaze fixed on the sandy, dun-streaked outcrop.

Sun glinted on silver.

As a loud *pop* sounded, he grabbed his twenty-four-inch, lever-actioned, blue steel barreled Winchester from its scabbard and threw himself out of the saddle. He aimed through the fixed-post frontsight and fired at the spot where he'd seen the flash.

Spooked, Eagle took off at a hard gallop.

The hombre or hombres returned fire. Hot lead bounced back and forth between them. A sharp sting pinged his arm and for a moment he thought he was hit. Then realized a bullet had found the side of the arroyo as rocks and pebbles rained down.

He aimed and pulled back the trigger. The chamber clicked empty. He was out of bullets. Hunkered down, he reloaded as lead continued to fly. He held his fire, unwilling to use all his ammo and waited.

Once again, sunlight gleamed on a rifle barrel.

Brandon fired.

"Earl." The shout echoed through the arroyo as a

large body fell spread-eagled to the rocky floor below where it landed with a thud.

Hunkered down, rifle still pointed upward, Brandon bided his time.

He didn't have to wait long. The sound of skittering hooves and shale sliding could be heard in the distance. Then galloping that grew fainter until it disappeared completely.

Still, he waited. It could be a trick. The other hombre could have sent Earl's horse scuttling down the trail and waited to finish off Brandon.

As close to the side as he could get, Brandon hunkered down. He stayed in place for over twenty minutes then decided the thinner man with the wild eyes didn't have the patience to wait any longer. His gaze on the ridge, he pushed up.

No shots broke the quiet. The wiry ambusher gone.

He strode to the body that had landed face down in the rocks and toed it over. The hombre dead as a door nail, his face unrecognizable.

He put fingers to his lips and let loose a shrill whistle.

No thud of hooves echoed in the stillness.

If Eagle didn't come back or if he didn't find water, he was in trouble.

He whistled again. Nothing but the rustle of a tumbleweed, as the wind blew it down the canyon, broke the silence.

He put his rifle over his shoulder and started walking.

CHAPTER 9

Stars winked in an ebony sky while orange embers shot into the heavens to meet them.

The smell of roasting rabbit made Alex's mouth water, as she shifted on a rough-barked log, slopping hot coffee over the side of her tin cup. Manuel had insisted on fixing the meal. He'd gotten no arguments from her or Charlie. Both exhausted.

She gave a surreptitious rub to her leg where the cat had scratched it when it lunged for her.

Tired beyond belief, every bone in her body aching, she plopped down her tin cup and sank to the ground, ignoring the various points of contact from small sharp stones. Even the enticing aroma of a hot meal couldn't quell the overwhelming fatigue.

"Meez Alex, you need to eat." Manuel brought her a plate with a roasted rabbit leg and hardtack on it.

"Tomorrow," she mumbled. "I'll eat it tomorrow."

Ignoring her growling stomach, she drifted off before she heard his reply, nor was even aware she whispered, "Brandon," before tumbling into deep, much needed sleep.

Scents she'd went to sleep to woke her. Opening her eyes, she looked into Manuel's brown ones. He squatted beside her, holding cup and plate. A deep pearly gray and coral sky coated the base of the horizon pink, and haloed the lean body of the young man crouched beside her.

"How are you feeling, Meez Alex?"

"I'm fine." She gave him a reassuring smile. Sleep had done her wonders. "What about you? You've been traveling nonstop for a while now."

"I come from hardy stock. I can handle a little time on horseback." He grinned at her.

She grinned back and accepted the plate. "Thanks for this."

"You are welcome."

As she bit into her hardtack, Charlie came striding out of the underbrush.

"Where's your sling?" she asked after swallowing the bite of biscuit.

"Chucked it in the brush. Don't need it."

~*~

Alex breathed in short, shallow breaths. Her muscles taut.

They were on their horses and traveling south, the pink disappearing from the sky, leaving leaden-blue, thick with heat and low-lying clouds.

Manuel halted, raising his hand. Charlie and Alex reined in beside him, and looked down. And then down some more.

Alex swallowed or tried to. Every bit of spit in her mouth gone. This was the worst part of the trip. She'd rather face a band of Comancheros than cross the narrow path, that she and Brandon had dubbed the

Narrow Divide. A canyon wall rose straight up on one side and dropped down into nothingness on the other. By the green shade of Manuel's face, she could tell he wasn't looking forward to it any more than she was. Charlie's expression stoic.

Dancer snorted, tossing his head up and down and dancing, restive.

She patted his neck and whispered, "I'm not thrilled about it either."

She threw another furtive glance at her companions. Beads of sweat stood out on Manuel's forehead. His eyebrows were elevated and his pecan-colored skin had a greenish hue to it, that clashed with his vibrant poncho. "It was brave of you to come and get us, Manuel." Alex spoke the truth. To do something that terrified you was the definition of bravery in her book.

He gave her a grateful smile, though the green in his face didn't lessen. "We'll"—the word came out a squawk. He swallowed and tried again. "We'll have to walk the horses."

"Agreed and remembered." She nodded. "Charlie, you want to lead and I'll bring up the rear."

He studied Manuel's frozen features then swung out of the saddle. "That might be best."

Shards of shale and pebbles, dislodged by large hooves, tumbled down the side of the mountain as, leading his horse, Charlie started across. Coaxing with gentle words when the horse nickered nervously. His voice and firm hand on the reins, the only thing keeping the mare from bolting.

A large stone bounced down the canyon wall just

as Charlie and his horse scrambled to the other side where the trail widened. The cowpuncher took off his hat, wiped his sweaty brow, then shoved it back on his head and nodded to Manuel.

His lips in a straight line, flesh stretched tight over bone, Manuel dismounted. Legs stiff, the young man started across.

He'd made it nearly halfway when the wind picked up. Thick hot air circled and whined, pushing against him, flattening his poncho to his angular frame. Sand and stone loosened as he pressed against the rocky face of the mountain, clutching at rough gray out-croppings of rock with one hand, the reins of his horse in the other.

Already nervy, sensing his rider's fear, the pinto reared, jerking the reins from Manuel's hand. Manuel lost his balance. His boot slid over the ledge, then the space he was balanced on collapsed and he fell back-ward.

Alex bit back the scream scraping her throat as he managed to claw a hold on the side of the mountain, his head visible, the rest of his body suspended in mid-air.

The pinto bolted. The horse's back hoof scraping Manuel's finger. Manuel let go and dropped another inch, now hanging by one hand.

Alex leaped forward. Pebbles rolled beneath one of her heels. She lost her balance and her right boot met air.

"Pull up and balance yourself, Young Alex. You can't help the boy from the bottom of the ravine,"

Charlie said, his voice calm.

Her heart pounding, drops of perspiration running down her face and into her eyes, she pulled her foot back and crab-walked to Manuel. Carefully, she lowered herself to the trail and grabbed his hand with both of hers. "I've got you."

The whites of his eyes gleaming, Manuel gave her a tight smile, his lips seamed together.

The pinto went galloping across the divide throwing debris under its hooves as it reached the other side.

As soon as the horse was out of the way, Charlie started back across.

Manuel's fingers slipped as rocks crumbled beneath them.

"Hold on. Hold on." She tightened her grip. Manuel had a good forty pounds on her. She wouldn't be able to hold him. If he went, they'd both go.

His fingers continued to slip.

"Hold on, hold on," she whispered again, the spit in her mouth gone.

"I can't. Let go, Meez Alex. I won't take you with me."

"I couldn't if I wanted to." She gave a dry laugh, her fingers frozen around his wrist.

He slipped another half-inch. Pain shot through her arms as she strained to hold on, digging into the shale and dirt with the toes of her boots. He dropped again, this time dragging her till her shoulders and chest were over the edge. Her breath came in short, harsh pants as she fought off lightheadedness. Her arms now shrieking. Her sockets ready to pop.

"Back up, Young Alex, I've got him." Charlie lay down on the trail. His hands under Manuel's armpits, he began to haul him up.

"Use your feet, boy, and your hands, chin if you have to, but hie yourself back on this ledge."

As he moved steadily upward, Alex let go of his hand and grabbed his arm, pulling. Manuel came tumbling over the side. A kick of his boot to her jaw sent her skittering backwards.

"Can you stand, boy?" Breathing heavily, Charlie pushed to his feet, rubbing his shoulder. Manuel sprawled face down on the trail. Alex on her hands and knees a few inches behind him.

Trembling, Manuel pushed to his knees, clutching the rocky face, then slowly rose to his feet.

"Young Alex?"

"I just might crawl across if it's all the same to you." But even as she said it, she was climbing to her feet and like Manuel clutched the side of the mountain.

Cautiously, they inched across. First Charlie, then Manuel. As her foot slipped on the last step, both men grabbed an arm and hauled her across.

Dancer trumpeted from the opposite side.

"Come on, boy."

The stallion shook its large head.

"You've got this, Dancer," she called.

The horse huffed then started across.

Manuel watched in disbelief.

Charlie noticed. "Oh, this is nothing. That hoss

once stomped a rattlesnake to death that had threatened Young Alex."

Manuel's jaw dropped.

Alex paid little heed, all her concentration on the big beautiful animal picking its way along a trail too narrow for the horse's large body. Stones tumbled beneath huge hooves as the stallion moved forward, throwing its head and swishing its tail.

The stallion was over halfway across when it stepped on a dragging rein. Alex's heart leaped to her throat and she took an involuntary step forward as Dancer sidled,back hoof meeting air.

Charlie clamped a hard hand on her arm.

"Let me go." She yanked her arm out of his grasp and started forward then stopped as the horse regained its footing and came bolting down the trail. She moved backward never taking her eyes off the stallion.

"That's the way, Dancer." She called out her encouragement. When her heel hit the widened portion of the trail, Charlie jerked her out of the path of the big stallion barreling toward them.

Dancer came thundering across. When the stallion stopped, she threw her arms around the foam-flecked neck and leaned her cheek against her horse. "You did it, Dancer."

The stallion snorted then nuzzled her.

She pulled a shriveled carrot out of her vest pocket, broke off a small piece and held it out for Dancer to crunch on. "When we get to a trading post, I'll buy you some sugar lumps." She patted the stallion's damp neck then turned to her companions. "Is every-one alright?"

Manuel nodded as he stuck his hand behind him, his face pale and drawn.

"Let's see your hand, Manuel," Alex commanded.

Reluctantly, he shoved it in front of him. The pinkie hung at an awkward angle where the pinto's hooves had caught it.

"We better get that set.

"Charlie, how's the shoulder?"

"It's still in its socket. While you see to his finger, I'll round up the horses." Not waiting for a reply, he trudged off.

She sighed, knowing it hurt like the devil, then turned her attention to the young Mexican. "I'm going to find a couple of twigs to set that finger with. You wait here."

In less time than she would have thought possible, they were back on the trail, their mounts collected, Manuel's finger set and, at her insistence, Charlie's arm once more in a sling.

Mile after mile, the horses trudged in the stifling heat. The afternoon long and wearing. As the sun dropped in a hazy sky, they topped a rise and reined in. Below them, in the middle of nowhere, sat two dilapidated buildings with horses tied out front.

CHAPTER 10

The sun beat down. Hot. Merciless.

Even Brandon's feet burned. Rocks and sand, scorching in their intensity, heated up the leather of his boots.

He stopped, put fingers to lips and whistled. Or tried to. His mouth, dry as parchment, produced more of a crow's squawk.

He waited and listened.

Nothing.

Swallowing as best he could, Brandon whistled again. This time the sound, louder and clearer.

He waited, listening. Not even the shriek of a hawk broke the silence. His heels sinking into sand, stumbling over an occasional rock, he strode on.

Once again, he put his fingers to his lips and whistled. This time not bothering to stop, barely listening for a response. And because he wasn't listening, he didn't hear it till it was too close to miss. The clip-clop of a horse's hooves moving at a steady trot. Rifle raised, he slid behind a boulder and waited.

A large roan trotted by, sand spurting under dark, hard hooves.

He cupped his hands and called, "Eagle."

Snorting, the horse stopped.

Brandon strode to the stallion, grabbed his canteen and took a healthy glug then poured some in one hand and gave it to the horse before climbing into the saddle.

As the sun lowered in the west, they continued southward, heading for the Rio Grande. He'd hoped Alex would leave some sign she'd been this way, but so far he'd seen nothing.

Eagle plodded on, lifting one large hoof after another, loosening pebbles, cracking the occasional twig and flattening craggy grass.

Leaning forward in the saddle, Brandon strained to get a glimpse of a gray-green ribbon of liquid that he needed to cross to get into Mexico.

Just as the sun wavered on the horizon, a winding band of pale silver glistened ahead. As if having done its duty, the sun sank with a rapidity that always managed to surprise. He wouldn't be crossing tonight, but at least they'd have water.

Brandon urged his big horse on, the sky still alive with purples and reds, and a band of orangey-gold hanging low on the horizon, that would soon disappear as quickly as the sun. As the stars came out, he heard the lap of water. Eagle's ears twitched and the horse broke into a gallop. They rode through trees and underbrush till the stallion halted and buried its nose in the rippling river. As the roan raised its head, water dripping off its velvet mouth, sky colors disappeared, replaced by ebony and diamond bright stars.

Brandon swung out of the saddle.

Crack. A twig snapped, loud in the silence. In one smooth motion he whirled, Peacemaker in hand.

A riderless buckskin came trotting out of the underbrush.

He stood motionless, listening, but no sound came except the snorting of the horses and the occasional buzz of an insect. He holstered his Colt Single Action Army, grabbed the reins of the buckskin and led it to the river to drink.

Gathering twigs, he built a fire and made coffee. As bright orange embers rose in the night sky, he pulled the saddles off both horses. As he sipped his coffee, he rifled through the saddlebags tossed over the back of the buckskin's saddle.

Hardtack, jerky, a couple of cans of peaches, coffee, and a spare break-action Smith and Wesson were snugged in the leather pouches. Running his hand over the smooth handle, he felt initials carved into it. Squinting, he held it up to the fire. E.L. It was looking more and more like the buckskin was Earl's mount and that the other rider had taken off for parts unknown. He placed Earl's supplies in his own bags then sat down to a meal of hardtack, jerky and peaches.

The fire crackled and the horses pulled and munched on wild grass while he ate. The familiar sounds soothing.

Finished with his meal, he leaned back against the saddle, pulled his hat over his eyes and spoke into the wind, "I'm coming, O'Malley. Stay out of trouble till I find you."

He slept restlessly and rose before dawn, rekindling the fire and reheating strong cold coffee, waiting for enough light to cross the Rio.

As the sky softened from jetty to pearly pink, he doused the fire and saddled his horse. Slowly, he made his way up and down the riverbank till he found the shortest crossing. A sandbar perched on the opposite side reached into the river. He hadn't crossed in this particular spot before and hoped it held no surprises.

Overhead, sullen clouds gathered. The color in the sky fading to ash.

With a tap of heels, Brandon nudged Eagle into the shallows. The water rose as huge hooves plopped against liquid soon up to Eagle's knees.

The buckskin, who'd tagged behind Eagle, trotted back and forth on the bank, neighing.

Eagle trumpeted.

"Don't encourage her," Brandon admonished.

The buckskin whinnied in response, continuing to trot up and down the bank. Then with a loud bugling call, and a spray of water, leaped into the shallows, surging through the water, drawing alongside them.

"You are on your own, horse." Brandon turned his attention to his mount.

The roan lifted long powerful legs, swimming strongly in churning water now up to the horse's withers. The buckskin struggled beside the stallion, nostrils flared, whites of eyes showing.

The horses continued moiling water beneath their hooves. Drawing closer and closer to the bank.

They were almost in the shallows when Brandon noticed the crumbling limestone along the riverbed. A quiver of unease rode his spine.

Eagle hit the shallows and began to trot forward, water spraying in colorful arcs, streaming off leather boots and chaps, turning them a dark, wet brown. Brandon's breath eased. They were nearly there.

Then, he heard a sucking noise and the buckskin screamed.

CHAPTER 11

The late afternoon sun broke through a hazy sheen, haloing large cactus and gleaming sand. Alex squinted through the mist at the two connected structures below, gray and faded from too much heat and not enough care. "Do you know anything about this place, Manuel?"

"It's frequented by bad men. Men who have nowhere else to go."

"Is one of those buildings a general store?"

"Of sorts. The other is a cantina. Much trouble erupts."

"We need supplies."

"Tomorrow we should be at the mission."

"Hopefully. But I'd like something to eat tonight. We finished the hardtack and jerky this morning." As if to emphasize her point her stomach growled loud and long.

"You do that on command?" Charlie asked, grinning.

"I'm hungry."

"I could scare up a rabbit."

"We're out of coffee." She knew that would seal the deal.

"Then let me ride down. If those men see you—"
The boy shuddered.

"Manuel, they could make mincemeat of any of us
if we go in alone. We go in together."

"Did you pack trousers?" Charlie asked. She was
currently wearing one of the split-skirts that Missus
Simms made her. This one old, tan and worn.

A look passed between them, both remembering
when she'd passed herself off as a boy.

"I did."

"Manuel, give her your poncho."

Twenty minutes later the horses trotted down the
slope. Alex in trousers, Manuel's multi-colored poncho and sombrero, a liberal sprinkling of dirt on her
face and her breasts bound.

"Just like old times, hey Charlie?" she said as they
loped down the sandy slope overlaid with scrub grass
and sagebrush.

He just shook his head. "Hope the boss don't fire
me for this."

"He won't. But if he did, I'd hire you back."

"Even if'n he did and you didn't. Wouldn't change
anything."

"I know, Charlie. You're a good friend." She reached
over and briefly put a hand on his arm.

"And you, Young Alex, if you'll pardon me saying
so, can always find a way to get into trouble."

Manuel looked shocked, but Alex just grinned.

They reined in, in front of the dilapidated building
on their left with a rough painted picture above the
door of a bag of flour, coffee beans and scattered soup

beans. The painted flour bag peeling.

"They don't have your touch with a paint brush," Charlie observed.

"Meez Alex—" Manuel began.

"For now, better shorten that to Alex," Charlie said.

Alex nodded her agreement.

She untied her paraffin-lined, wood canteen from the saddle horn, swung out of the saddle and led Dancer to the water trough that stood next to a water pump. As she loosened the reins to let her horse drink, a wizened little woman with skin as wrinkled and tough as old shoe leather stepped out of the store. She wore a dusty dress, that at one time might have been blue, but was now so washed out it was hard to tell. It had a high collar and dragged the ground at her feet. "That'll be two bits for each horse and two bits for each canteen."

"You—" Alex was so astonished, she momentarily forgot to deepen her voice. Then remembered, "charge for water?" she said in more husky tones.

"I just said so, didn't I?"

"That's robbery."

"You're in the right place for it, ain't ya?" The woman cackled showing two broken front teeth.

"And if I choose not to pay?"

"Carlos," she called over her shoulder.

The floor thudded as a hulking, mountain of a man stomped out of the store to stand behind the tiny woman. "This is my son. He don't talk much, but he's not stupid and he's good at following orders."

Alex blinked. She'd never seen anyone so big. He could make two of the three of them put together and still have room left over. It wasn't that he was fat. Not one bit. He was tall and muscled. Extremely muscled.

Without another word, Alex pulled coins out of her vest pocket and handed them to the woman.

"If you want supplies, they're in here." She jerked her head behind her. "If you want drinks, through there." She pointed at swinging doors with a faded beer glass painted over them. The foam washed-out. The gold brew now a sickly yellow.

Under the narrowed gaze of the big man watching them, they watered the horses, filled their canteens then went through the door with the flour sack pictured above it.

The boards creaked as Alex walked into the windowless, dim-lit store. Coated with dust, goods of all description and sizes set on shelves and on the floor. Coffee was behind the counter next to the beans and bullets.

"I'd like a sack of Cowboy Coffee and a pound of beans."

The woman thumped them down on the counter. "Anything else?"

"Sugar."

The woman turned and pulled down a loaf of hard sugar from the shelf behind her and sliced off a piece.

"Would you break it up?"

"It'll cost you."

"Of course it will," Alex said, resigned.

The old woman cut the loaf in bits and wrapped

them in blue paper.

"Two bits for the coffee. Two bits for the beans. Two for the sugar and a half dime for breaking it up."

Alex tossed down her coin.

Charlie stepped up beside her and pointed at the cardboard boxes of bullets, labeled .45 Colt. "I'll take two of those."

The bullets rattled as she plunked down the boxes.

"That's 50 rounds per box."

"How much?"

"Half eagle."

Alex bit back the chuckle tickling her throat as Charlie, grumbling under his breath, threw down a gold coin. Grabbing her sacks, she headed out just as Dancer trumpeted. She ran through the door in time to see a tall man wearing a faded green shirt and tan vest trying to grab the stallion's reins.

The big horse reared, flailing hooves knocking the hombre down. Dust rose as he hit the ground, hard.

He drew his gun.

"I wouldn't." Alex's purchases splatted at her feet as she whipped out her peacemaker.

Still on his back, the hombre turned his pistol on Alex.

Enraged, the black stallion once again rose on hind legs, powerful forelegs churning air, ready to strike.

"It's okay, boy." Alex spoke soothingly. "Now drop that gun before I drop you," she told the hombre.

A shot fired behind her. She whirled.

Another bandito lay on the ground, gun falling from slack fingers.

Charlie's pistol smoked in his hand. "Look out," he yelled and whirled in the direction of the would-be horse thief. The hombre rolled in the dirt just in time to miss Charlie's bullet and Dancer's hooves, his gun still aimed at Alex.

He cocked back the hammer.

Alex fired.

Dust billowed as he slumped in the dirt, blood pooling on his chest.

More men came tumbling out of the cantina, guns raised.

In three quick strides, Charlie stood beside Alex, shoulder to shoulder, guns drawn. Manuel stood a few paces away, pistol extended.

A bandito fired, missing all three of them and plugging a whole in the water trough. Liquid came gushing out, pooling in the dirt and sand.

Before they could return fire, the storekeep, now standing on the doorstep, a rusty rifle in her hands, said, "That's enough. You three get on your horses and head on out. You other gents, drag those carcasses away from my front door then either leave or step back in for a drink. Makes me no never mind, but there will be no more fighting at my establishment."

Her son stood behind her, carrying a business-looking Winchester.

Grumbling, most of the men headed back inside, while two went to haul away the bodies.

Alex, Charlie and Manuel grabbed their supplies, jumped on their horses and galloped away. Alex's shoulder blades quivering, expecting a bullet at any moment. She nudged Dancer into a run. Huge hooves spurt sand and an occasional pebble.

No shots rang out as they topped the rise, the old woman's word law among the lawless.

CHAPTER 12

Sinkhole!

With a loud splash, the buckskin's flanks dropped, back hooves sinking in wet, sucking sand as the horse frantically fought for purchase with flailing front hooves. The river water rising in dirty torrents as the mare floundered, pushing and pulling, digging into shifting sand and silt, screaming in panic. Eyes rolling, flashing white.

Jaw clenched, Brandon grabbed his lariat, twirled it then snaked it out, sending it swishing toward the buckskin. For a moment, it hovered over the horse's head. Then the wind picked up and gusted. The rope sailed over the mare and plopped in the water, sending drops splashing as the lariat smacked on choppy waves.

Cursing, Brandon drew it back in and once again circled the wet twisted fiber over his head and let it fly. Again, the wind, plastering his shirt against him, played havoc with his throw. With a splash, the rope plunked on the water, sending a small geyser of wet into the air.

This time he aimed for a spot to the right of the buckskin. The lariat hovered over the mare's head then slid down the animal's neck. He wrapped the other end of the rope around the saddle horn.

"Let's go," he shouted over the keening gusts. He clapped wet boots against wet sides and Eagle leaped forward. The mare whinnied and flung its head back and forth as the noose tightened. Eagle pushed on, deeper into the shallows. Nearly to the bank.

Hind end dancing, the mare tried to pull out of the deadly bog hole. Brandon kept the reins tight, inching Eagle forward a step at a time, afraid to put too much pressure on the buckskin's neck.

Then he heard it. A sucking sound. Mud and sand releasing its quarry.

The rope went slack and the buckskin leaped forward shooting past him.

His shoulders dropped and his jaw unclenched. Grinning from ear to ear, he unwound the lariat wrapped around the saddle horn and let the horse go. The mare galloped up the bank, only stopping when it reached dry ground. Head hanging. Water streaming.

Eagle clomped up beside the buckskin and nudged it.

The buckskin lifted its head and laid it tiredly over the stallion's neck. Brandon reached over and removed the rope digging into the horse's skin. Leaning back in the saddle, he studied the sky. The sun was now out, the clouds dissipated and the nemesis wind gone.

"Daylight's a wastin." He clucked to his horse. Eagle broke into an easy canter while the buckskin trotted tiredly beside the roan. "And they say, I had a way with the ladies." He patted his horse's neck.

Eagle snorted in response.

"No need to brag."

~*~

Brandon traveled through the afternoon. As the horses crossed a sandstone canyon, they began to prance and snort, their movements nervy. Brandon looked around, then up. On a rocky overhang, still as a statue, lurked a thin, tawny-colored puma. If the hanging nipples were anything to go by, the big cat had kits nearby. He rested his hand on his gun, keeping the puma in his sights. The chance of a cat attacking in broad daylight was slim, but he took nothing for granted. The puma stared down. Tension rose as minutes passed. Finally, with a twitch of its tail, the big cat limped away.

Brandon took his hand off his gun and they rode on. Through one canyon after another, into scrub grass, even at one point a thin stream no bigger than a ribbon that the horses could drink at and he could fill his canteens.

Then, come evening, as the sun was sinking behind the mountains, he hit the Narrow Divide.

CHAPTER 13

The wind whispered.

Throwing her hand over her head, she ignored it.

It came again.

She closed her eyes tighter.

It whispered again.

Yawning, Alex forced open eyes crusted with sleep. Her mind heavy with fatigue.

The sky lightened from deepest ebony to dark charcoal, stars growing dim as dawn approached.

"O'Malley."

No. Not the wind. Brandon. He'd found her. She stumbled to her feet. Joy coursed through her as she stared into the dark, quivering like a bloodhound that had caught scent. "Brandon," she whispered.

No response came.

Her shoulders drooped. It had been the wind or maybe a dream. Though, she could have sworn...

Charlie stirred. "You okay, Young Alex?" She might be Mrs. Wade to those that didn't know her but to Charlie who'd rode beside her on the cattle drive she'd always be Young Alex.

"A dream. I was dreaming." Though, it'd felt so real. She'd heard the whiskey-smooth tones of her husband. Could almost feel his warm, hard-muscled arms wrapped around her.

"Must have been a doozy."

"Yeah."

"Dawn's coming. I'll build a fire and put coffee on."

"Thanks, Charlie."

~*~

As the sun came up and the sky lightened in a veritable display of color, the little party set out on the last leg of their journey. Today, barring no unforeseen circumstances, they would reach the mission.

Nerves jumped under Alex's skin, warring with excitement. It would be wonderful to see the Sisters Marie and Sarah, Father Jon and the children again.

But smallpox. Her belly clinched.

Besides snakes, not much scared her. The disease though was another matter. Smallpox was a killer. When she was growing up, it had decimated the town she lived near, including her best friend. There'd been no doctor, let alone vaccines, available. The town and her family's ranch too remote.

She shuddered. It had been a scary time and she'd never quite got over the fear of wondering if she'd be next. Luckily, her mother had done her level best to keep them safe, including making them wear scarfs over their nose and mouth whenever they were in public. And constantly washing their hands till they were raw. At the time, she'd thought it was silly. But the family had escaped the dread disease.

And now, years later, smallpox once more threatened. The vaccines still hadn't made their way to remote areas in Mexico and the West.

Straightening her spine, she sat tall in the saddle. She'd survived it once and would again, and hopefully save lives in the process. And when she got back home, she'd have Brandon talk to his friends back East about getting the serum sent to Silverhills and inoculating everyone on the ranch. He had tried, at least once before, but for whatever reason, they hadn't received the serum.

Well, nothing she could do about that now. She shifted her attention to her surroundings and just in time, as Dancer shifted to the left to avoid the cylindrical stems and barbed spines of a Jumping Cholla Cactus. Better known as the Devil's Cactus because of its nasty habit of launching those dangerous spikes into tender flesh.

The day wore on. The sky grew heavy. The air filled with misty rain and the scent of dank earth.

Alex pulled down her cowboy hat and pulled up the collar of her slicker. The horses slogged through soil with more loam than sand. Up rises and down. Then vegetation grew sparse. Sand reappeared. Gray tumbleweeds leaned up against giant sage-colored cactus that reached for the sky. Their needles long. Deadly. Still, the trio plodded on, not bothering to speak as the emerging sun sucked up every bit of moisture. Every bit of energy.

Finally, as the sky continued to darken and evening approached, they arrived at the mission.

Charlie started to dismount.

"Charlie, wait."

He hung suspended for a moment then settled back into the saddle. Warm leather creaking beneath him. He gave her an inquiring look then his gaze sharpened as he read something in her eyes. "Don't say it. The answer's no."

Manuel's head swung back and forth between the two, his eyebrows raised, his gaze questioning.

"I'm going in with you. I didn't sign on to wait in town."

"I'm not going to put you at risk." She raised her chin, determined. Giving him stare for stare. Why did every man she knew, with the possible exception of Manuel and Father Jon, have to be so bullheaded?

"That's not your decision to make."

"It's an order, Charlie." Sensing her tension, Dancer moved restively beneath her.

"Feel free to fire me, but I'm going with you." His stubbly, square jaw set at a mulish angle.

"Charlie—"

"I'm going in the mission with you."

She studied him quietly then said, "If something goes awry, who's going to take me home?"

His expression changed to one of pained comprehension. "Manuel." But his voice lacked conviction.

"It's not Manuel's place."

Manuel opened his mouth to protest. Alex quelled him with a look.

Charlie's face reflected his struggle. He squirmed in the saddle, trying to find a way around the unthinkable.

"I'd want to be buried at Siverhills. Where I could

hear the whicker of horses and lowing of cattle. Not miles from my home." And Silverhills was home. It had been since the first moment she looked down from a rise that sparked and glistened when the sun hit it, to the bustling community below, and knew she was where she belonged.

"I see now how you always manage to get around the boss." He sighed heavily, fidgeting in the saddle. "Know this. I will be camped right outside the gate. Day and night."

"Why, don't you go home with Manuel? You can still check on me daily."

"That's the deal. Take it or leave it."

"Where will you sleep?" She looked around uneasily. There was no shelter. They were on the outskirts of town, but still that was a quarter mile away.

Manuel spoke up. "My cousin owns a cantina, in the village, that he sells supplies out of. He has an old chuckwagon he uses for supply runs. He may be persuaded to rent it to you. Charlie can get his water from the village well and buy provisions at the cantina. I will stay with him."

"Not necessary," Charlie said.

"I will stay with you," Manuel repeated, his chin raised, his decision made.

"Thank you, Manuel. Tell him to name his price. I'll pay whatever he asks," Alexandria said. "In fact, why don't we do that now?"

"We can handle this, Meez Alex. There will be much haggling involved. It will take many hours. You never offer top dollar to begin with. Why don't you go ahead and settle in?"

She smiled at the idea of the haggling. Then another thought hit her. "Will the villagers give you any problems because of your mother and sister helping smallpox victims?"

"They know I've been gone for several weeks. I can't possibly infect them."

"Alright. I hope they see it that way. People go a little crazy when they fear something. Just be careful."

While the men waited, she jumped off Dancer. The mission sat behind a sturdy sandstone wall, the color faded to a rich warm yellowish-brown. A wide wooden door with an iron handle and bell-pull attached was the only way in.

Alex pulled the handle. As expected, it was locked. She then rang the bell. Waited several minutes, then rang it again. She turned to the two men. "Go get the wagon. I'll be fine."

Neither made a move to leave.

She shrugged and again pulled the rope the bell was attached to. This time giving it several brisk tugs. The bell jangled loudly.

An unfamiliar voice responded, "We have smallpox here. Whoever you are you'd best ride on."

CHAPTER 14

Color filled the evening sky as the sun hovered on the horizon. Bright purples and crimson reds, with strips of rosy peach, glistened off the canyon walls. A lone coyote howled in the distance, making the horses snort and sending a quiver of unease down Brandon's spine as he stared at the sheer drop that ended on a rocky floor below. Promising certain death to anyone who went over. He'd reached the Narrow Divide, as he and Alexandria referred to the pencil thin ledge.

The sun took another dip and the canyon darkened. Both ends of the gorge below impassable with rock, pine and scrub.

This was it. Either he crossed now or waited till morning.

No point in putting it off. He swung out of the saddle and, with the reins in his right hand, started across a narrow trail at the huge canyon's edge that would eventually widen and slope back down to the desert. A rider could go around it but it would add days to the journey. Days Brandon couldn't afford.

The mare nickered in distress, pacing the stony outcropping he'd just left. Eagle whinnied in response. The clip-clop of hooves echoing on the narrow rocky ledge.

"Keep your mind on what you're doing. She's either coming or she's not."

The roan took two more steps then came to a stiff-legged halt, jerking Brandon's arm, pulling him around. His heel hit crumbling shale and for one brief moment, he lost his footing. He grabbed the side of the mountain and pulled his foot back, breathing heavily, cold beads of sweat popping on his forehead.

"What in thunder?" Angry, he jerked on the reins then saw the whites of Eagle's eyes. The stallion was spooked and it had nothing to do with the mare.

Rattle-rattle-rattle.

His lips thinned and his heart rate jacked up. He took a long sweeping gaze at the trail.

Three feet away, blending with the gloom and soaking up the heat from the rocky structure, sat a rattler.

Brandon stood motionless. Maybe it would head back the way it had come.

The tail began to twitch and rattle again. The head raised and the narrow, forked tongue came out.

Maybe not.

With slow, careful movements, he knotted the reins and drew them over Eagle's head, freeing his hands. Degree by degree, he drew his gun.

Shadows were lengthening. He had to get off this ledge. The mare whinnied again, disturbing the snake further.

Rattle. Rattle. Rattle.

Brandon aimed and fired. The gunshot boomed,

hitting the snake. The reptile bounced into the air then disappeared over the divide. Behind it, rock crumbled. A shudder traveled up the side of the ledge.

They had to get moving. Now! He grabbed the reins and started forward. Deepening shadows making it hard to see what lay ahead.

His boot sank in shale loosened from his shot, sending pebbles and rocks tumbling over the side. He pulled his foot up and took a wide step forward, rocks bouncing over the edge behind him, guiding Eagle with the reins.

They moved swiftly.

Almost there. Twenty steps, fifteen, ten...

A small boulder, sitting precariously on the edge of the ledge above, loosened by the shot and quiver of the mountainside, rumbled overhead then came tumbling.

Man and horse shot forward and kept going.

The ground widened beneath them. They'd made it.

Brandon wiped his damp brow.

He looked back in the gloom where the mare paced nervously on the other side of the divide. Eagle whinnied.

The mare trumpeted back.

Hooves rang on rock as the buckskin came galloping across. Closer and closer, charging toward them.

The mare stumbled on the shallow indention Brandon's bullet had made. Brandon's heart caught as a back hoof went over the edge.

The mare shrieked.

Then the horse was up and moving forward, hooves soaring, pebbles and rocks flying. As the sun disappeared on the horizon, and darkness closed in, the buckskin bolted off the divide and onto solid ground.

He patted the animal's wet neck as the mare stood head down and quivering. "Good job, hoss. Good job."

Grabbing Eagle's bridle, he led the horse away from the ledge, the buckskin clip-clopping behind. He shook his head. Of everything he'd expected to encounter on this journey, horse love hadn't been on the list.

Brandon made camp. Built a fire and put on the coffee. He opened the second tin of peaches he'd found in Earl's back pack with his knife, extending his meal of hardtack and jerky. Leaning back against his saddle, gulping down the strong dark liquid in his dented cup, he watched the orange embers crackle and burn, winding their way upwards, only to turn into ash and float back down, and wondered for the thousandth time if his wife was safe.

"I'm coming, O'Malley," he whispered his nightly mantra, then tossed the remains of his coffee on the ground and settled down to get some much-needed shuteye.

He slept fitfully and awoke with a start. Senses alert, he took a hard look around. It wasn't the lightening of the sky that woke him. What had? Then he heard it. The sounds of boot heels and the clip-clop of a horse's hooves coming across the divide.

The buckskin whickered and trotted out to meet

the newcomer or more accurately the newcomer's horse as Brandon melted into the trees.

"So, this is where you got to," the rider murmured.

Shifty Eyes, the other hombre who'd tried to kill him, rode into camp.

"I know you're out there. Come out where I can see you," Shifty Eyes called out, his six-gun extended.

Peacemaker drawn, Brandon stepped out of the shadows.

CHAPTER 15

The setting sun hit the old bell hanging in the belfry with blinding intensity then abruptly dropped below the horizon. The bright colors left in its wake changing from purple and red to a pale gray that muted popping stars.

"I've come to help." Alex raised her voice to be heard through the thick door.

"That's mighty kind of you, I'm sure. But you don't want no part of what's on this side of the door." The husky voice sounded unbearably weary.

"This is Alexandria O'Malley. Please tell Father Jon or the good sisters I'm here."

"There's only one sister left."

Alex's breath caught and she had to lock her knees to keep them from buckling. "Which—" The word came out in a raspy whisper. She cleared her throat and tried again. "Which one?"

"Which one did the angels take or is still with us?"

"Just tell me, dammit."

"Sister Sarah died two days ago."

Alex leaned her head against the door. Her heart leaden. Grief threatening to overwhelm her.

"What of my mother and sister?" Manuel called,

anxiety on his face and in his voice.

"Manuel. Is that you?"

"Yes, Meez Rosie."

"I thought you were bringing back a doctor."

"I tried. There were none. At least, none that would come. I thought Meez Alex might know of someone. I hadn't expected her to come herself. Though I should have," he added. "How is my sister and mother?"

"I'm sorry to say, they have both come down with the contagion."

"I must see them. Help them." He threw himself off his horse and went racing toward the gate.

"No. That is exactly what you mustn't do. It would just upset them. Now I'm going to get Father Jon. He can decide what's to be done."

"Meez Rosie."

No response.

"Meez Rosie," he yelled, panic roiling off him, in the beads of sweat on his brow and the high-pitched edge to his voice.

He heaved a sigh. Rosie was no longer at the gate.

Her heart still twisted in her chest, Alex forced her shoulders to straighten. "When did Rosie arrive, Manuel?"

He didn't respond.

"Manuel."

"Yes?" He turned and looked at her.

"When did Rosie arrive?"

"A few days before the contagion broke out. She came to get her nephew."

"Young Alex, maybe we should—"

"Don't say it, Charlie," Alex interrupted. "They are shorthanded as it is. Especially now," her voice trailed off.

Before Charlie could respond, an old familiar voice sounded from the other side of the door, filled with sorrow and fatigue. "Alexandria, is that you?"

"Father Jon!" She hastily pulled her red bandana over her mouth and nose. The gate creaked as he opened it a crack.

"He's aged ten years," was her first thought. Like her, his mouth was covered with cloth. His, a strip of thick white cotton. The Father's eyes were red-rimmed and dull, scoured lines at their edges. What was visible of his skin, tinged with gray. His normally-crisp black cassock hung limp on stooped shoulders, one of its thirty-three buttons representing Christ's earthly life, missing.

"What are you doing here?"

"Father Jon, how is my family?" Manuel interrupted pressing up against the door.

"They're holding their own."

"Let me in. I must see them."

"They wouldn't want that, my son."

Before Manuel could say anything more, Father Jon spoke to Alex and asked again, "What are you doing here?"

"I came to help."

"No. I can't let you do that." He gave a tired shake of his head. His gaze shifted and he looked at Manuel. "I thought you were bringing back a doctor."

"I couldn't find anyone willing to come. I thought Meez Alex might know of someone so I went to Silverhills." He shrugged.

"I insisted on coming over Manuel's objections."

Once more, Father Jon's gaze traveled around the outside of the mission. "Where is your husband?"

"On a trail drive."

"So he doesn't know you came."

"He will by now."

"Thank you for coming. It shows a huge heart, loyalty and compassion, but I can't let you in."

"Father Jon, just who do you have to help you?"

"Sister Marie. And Rosie. Sister Sarah passed." Pain sounded in his voice, sorrow shown in his eyes.

"I'm so very saddened to hear that."

"Thank you. Now you must go."

"Let me in, Father. I am not leaving you and Sister Marie on your own. You took me in, in my hour of need. Now I'm repaying my debt."

"Think of your children."

"I am. And what I'm thinking is they wouldn't be alive today if you hadn't taken me in."

"Is there anything I can say to make you change your mind?" His eyes careworn.

"No."

Silence stretched, hanging heavy in the stifling air, as Father Jon weighed his options. Their gazes locked. Tension built.

Did the good Father really think a little thing like a closed gate was going to keep her out?

CHAPTER 16

Guns drawn, Brandon and Shifty Eyes faced each other across the campfire. Night pressed in. Heavy. Oppressive. Whites of eyes eerie in firelight.

"I should have killed you when I had the chance." Thin lips lifted in a sneer. The voice filled with hate. "You killed my brother."

"If you're expecting condolences, it ain't a gonna happen." Brandon stood straight, his shoulders squared, his legs splayed, his mind focused. No emotion clouded his judgement. Brother or no brother, both men were killers. And this one was gonna try to take him down.

"Why you—" Shifty Eyes' finger tightened on the trigger.

Too late.

The acrid smell of sulphur rose from Brandon's smoking gun. Shifty Eyes' shot went wild as he slowly slumped then fell from his saddle.

Brandon removed the saddle and bridle from the chestnut mare the hombre had rode, kicked the body into the underbrush and fell into exhausted slumber.

~*~

He was in the saddle and heading south as the

sun broke on the horizon, pushing back the night with streaks of pink and gold, illuming saguaro cactus over twenty feet tall. Bronzing chollas' barbed spines that could impale man or beast. Intensifying the acrid scent of sagebrush in the hot, still air.

Eagle kept up a mile-eating trot while the buckskin cantered behind. Shifty Eyes' chestnut having taken off for parts unknown.

By midafternoon, he rounded a rise with some greenish-gray grass growing on it. Mexican bush sage's purple blooms adding color to the barren surroundings. He reined in. Below him, two dilapidated gray buildings sagged against each other.

Nudging Eagle with his heels, he headed down the hill, sand kicking up and swirling beneath the horses' huge hooves.

He tied Eagle to the hitching post, leaving enough room for the horse to reach the trough. The buckskin sidled up to the roan and dunked its nose in the tepid water.

A middle-aged man with a thin mustache and graying stubble on his jaw strode out of the swinging doors of the cantina, his heels clicking. He wore a multi-colored, dusty serape and a black sombrero. Taking one look at the buckskin, saddleless and sans a bridle, he said, "Where'd you find my horse?"

"Your horse?" Brandon gave him a cool look.

"Yeah, my horse. It wandered off a couple of days ago."

"Mister, that's not your horse."

"I'm saying it is and that you're trying to steal her.

We don't take kindly to horse thieves here."

Other men had gathered at the doorway, watching.

Smirking, the man started toward the buckskin.

"I know it's not your horse. You want to know how?"

Brandon's words stopped him in midstride. Still full of bravado, he said, "Tell me why it ain't my horse."

"Because I killed the man that was riding it." Brandon stared straight at the hombre, his hand on his gun, his face hard.

The hombre gave a visible gulp. "Now that you mention it, I don't think that's my horse after all."

Brandon nodded, and shoved his way through the crowd gathered at the door. The men parted, murmuring, as he strode to the bar.

Except for the sun pouring through the swinging doors, the room was shadowed and dark. The bar scarred and ridged with rings from beer and whiskey glasses that had sweat then dried onto the counter. The stock behind the bar layered with dust and smudged by oily fingerprints.

One of the biggest men Brandon had ever seen stood behind the long rail serving. He wore a dirty tan shirt. A stained apron strained around his middle.

The men who'd crowded around the door strolled back in. Two heading to the bar. Four others sat down at a table with cards and chips on it. The cards face down. A young woman who'd been sitting at the table got up with a swish of skirts. Her dress red and tight-fitting at the bust and waist. Hoops dangled at her ears. Heavy makeup covered a pretty face.

She sidled up to him and gave him a flirtatious smile. "Buy me a drink?"

He nodded to the bartender and tossed down two-bits.

"If you watered your horse that will be another two-bits."

"You got to be kidding me."

"We never joke about money here."

Brandon rolled his eyes and tossed down coin.

"You want something to drink?" the bartender asked in a deep, gruff voice.

Brandon took in the dirt on the floor and the grime in the cracks and crevices of the bar and said, "Beer." He reached in his pocket and tossed down another coin.

As he glanced around, he noticed a leathery old woman standing in the doorway that divided the two buildings.

The bartender thumped a watery-looking brew down in front of him that spilled over the sides of the dirty glass.

"Any strangers been in here?" He divided the question equally between the bartender and the girl.

The bartender ignored the question and walked to the other end of the bar to serve two cowboys huddled there. Sipping their brew, watching him, their gazes both curious and suspicious.

He turned his attention to the girl and repeated, "Seen any strangers here lately? In the last week or so?"

She stepped into his space, putting a hand on his arm, her scent of cheap perfume and body odor overwhelming. "Now, honey, you want to talk or you want some action?"

He pulled out a double eagle and laid it on the counter. "I want to talk."

She gave him a puzzled frown. Apparently, that wasn't the answer she was used to.

The bartender came lumbering back.

"We don't take much to strangers that ask questions here."

The room quieted.

Hot, tired and sick with worry, he drew back his lips in what was supposed to pass for a smile. Though the barkeep would remark later it was more like a wolf extending its fangs. He lifted his fists to the giant behind the bar, needing to work off the anxiety that constantly crawled under his skin.

"What are you going to do about it?" His voice soft, heat sparked behind his eyes. The room grew quiet.

"There will be no brawling in my saloon today." The wizened little woman dressed in dusty black, gray hair escaping an unkept bun, strode forward decisively. Small, worn black boots peeked from beneath the dress and clicked as she crossed the room.

She came to a stop in front of Brandon and pointed a finger at him. "You. Come with me."

Brandon clenched and unclenched his fists. Fighting the overpowering urge to pound on somebody. And the barkeep was just what he needed to work off his aggressive tendencies.

"Aw Maw."

Brandon blinked. That mountain came out of that skinny little woman? Nature was something for sure.

"Don't you Aw Maw me."

She motioned with a finger for Brandon to follow her and marched out of the barroom, crossed the threshold and entered a darkened store. Brandon heaved a defeated sigh and followed her. She stopped in front of a row of dusty flour sacks and coffee bean bags, and looked him up and down. "You should be thanking me. If my son had gotten hold of you, that pretty face of yours wouldn't been pretty much longer."

He gave her an offended look, which she ignored. "Now, you want information on strangers that's been through here?"

"Most definitely." He straightened all thoughts of fighting forgotten.

"It'll cost you another double eagle like you gave the girl in there."

"And how much of that does she get to keep?" He gave her a level look.

"Oh, I might take two bits off the top. Goes toward her room and board." She pointed at rickety stairs that led to the second floor. "But for the most part, it's hers."

"Why you're just a fount of good works." Brandon's voice leaden with sarcasm. The girl was young. Way too young to be plying the oldest trade in the world.

"No. That I'm not. What I am is a business

woman." She held out her hand. He dropped a double eagle in it.

"About a week ago, three strangers stopped in. More interested in supplies than drinks."

Brandon's heartbeat quickened and he leaned forward. Intent on what she had to say.

"What did they look like?"

"One was a young Mexican. One a cowpoke and the other wore a serape and sombrero with a face liberally coated in dirt. Hair up under the hat. Not a bad disguise."

"Were they in good health?" His voice came out strained and he pushed the words from a raw throat.

"She your woman?"

"Were they in good health?" He ignored her question.

"Since you already gave me a double eagle, I'll just charge you two bits for that piece of information."

He dug out a coin and flipped it to her. She caught it deftly and slid it in her pocket where it joined the double eagle he'd already given her.

"Your woman appeared fine."

The air whished out of his lungs and he locked his legs to keep from sagging with relief.

"Thank you," he said sincerely.

"If you want to thank me, buy something."

"You're wasted here. You'd make a killing in St. Louie."

"I am indeed. And yes, I would." She gave a rusty cackle.

He grabbed a bag of coffee, and a bag of oats for

the horses, tossed her more coin, then threw down another double eagle.

"What's the eagle for?"

"The young girl's room and board." Then he strode out of the musty store into the clean and arid air of outdoors. His heart lighter. O'Malley was okay.

At least she was a week ago.

CHAPTER 17

"Fath—" Alex began.

The gate creaked open.

With a heavy sigh, Father Jon took a step back.

Sand shifted beneath worn boots as Charlie strode forward.

Before he could reach her, Alex led Dancer through the gate, closed it, and shot the bolt. "Go get that wagon," she shouted.

"You're awfully stubborn, Young Alex." Charlie stood nose to nose with the bolted gate. "Stay safe," he added, his voice gruff.

"You too, Charlie." She put her hand on the rough wood as if somehow, by that physical act, she could connect with her friend on the other side, borrow a little of his quiet strength. Taking a deep breath and straightening her shoulders, she turned, tied the reins around Dancer's neck to let the horse wander around the confines of the mission then hurtled after the disappearing cassock.

Entering the mission building, she strode down the tan adobe floor, a wooden crucifix hanging on the right wall, a picture of the Madonna on the left. Heels clicking, she turned the corner in time to see the black cassock disappear around the corner. The priest stood waiting for her at a worn wooden door that she remembered opened into the sick bay.

"Last chance to turn back," he said as she came to a halt beside him.

Even through the door she could smell the sweet, pungent scent of sick and worse yet, the rancid scent of death.

For one overwhelming moment, she thought about doing just that, turning tail and running. Away from sickness. Away from death.

She straightened her shoulders and found her momentarily misplaced backbone. Even so, all she could do was shake her head, her throat too dry to respond.

His dark cassock rustled. He fingered the wooden cross at his neck then threw open the door.

It was worse, much worse, than anything she'd imagined.

Row upon row of beds filled with sick children and two women, one middle-aged, one in her teens, that she took to be Manuel's family, lined the hot room.

Sister Marie was making the sign of the cross with one hand and pulling up the sheet on a small form with another.

A woman she didn't know was holding the hand of a young boy that stared sightlessly in front of him.

All around children moaned, in different stages of the grim disease, many with scabs covering their bodies. Her gaze slid from one bed to another, her throat dry, her lungs refusing to expel air. What made her think she could help these innocents, when death had already marked them?

Her hands fisted. Her stomach knotted and bile rose in her throat. For one brief moment, she thought she would heave her stomach's contents. She swallowed hard, straightened her shoulders, and lifted her chin. She could make a difference and she would. "What can I do to help?"

The light that always shone out of Father Jon's brown eyes had dimmed. Resignation and weariness coated him like fine-grained dust. His shoulders slumped. "Rosie," he pointed at the woman holding the small boy's hand, "is doing our cooking. Sister Marie takes care of the sick. You can help me bury the dead."

~*~

Digging up the sandy ground had been easy compared to lowering a tiny lifeless body into it.

While insects chittered in the background, they buried the little girl by lantern light where too many others lay. In the distance, a coyote howled. A lonely, sad sound as if the animal itself was bemoaning the loss of life for one so young.

Leaving Father Jon praying over the gravesite, she stumbled into the dark and climbed up the steps to the belfry where she could look down at the town.

She stared at the dark streets, where only a flickering candle in an occasional small adobe dwelling broke the dark. Even the moon was in hiding. Dark, sullen clouds hanging low in the sky.

For a long time, she'd traveled alone with only

Mongrel and Dancer for company. Then Brandon had erupted into her life. Or more accurately, she'd erupted into his. She'd gotten used to his vibrant company and the hustle and bustle of the ranch. Was as dependent on it as the air she breathed. And now. Here. There was so much quiet. So much heartbreak. And beneath that, a gathering tension—and fear.

From the opposite end of the narrow, winding street, a horse's nicker broke the quiet. She squinted, trying to see through the gloom. A white shape rolled down the earth-packed track, hardened by feet, hooves and spoked-wheels. As it got closer to the mission, she made out the outline of a chuckwagon being drawn by two shadowy riders.

Her heart eased. She might not have Brandon at her side, but she had a friend, a piece of Silverhills.

Quietly, she made her way down the winding wooden stairs of the belfry to sick bay where she helped Sister Marie till well past midnight then fell into her assigned cot in the room she shared with Rosie and Sister Marie, and into exhausted slumber.

The next morning, she got up and helped in the sick bay again. And again. One day leached into another and another till a week had passed. Each night before bedtime, she climbed the steps leading to the belfry where she looked down to make sure Charlie and Manuel where well. Their wagon parked next to the gate, like a sentinel. After assuring herself they were alright, her gaze automatically turned north as if following the lodestar. She waited and when she finally turned away, she repeated the same mantra,

"Tomorrow. Brandon will come tomorrow."

More days passed.

And then came the unthinkable.

She'd felt uneasy all day. Maybe because the air was thick and oppressive as if a storm was brewing. She didn't wait till bedtime but climbed the stairs of the belfry at sunset.

As she reached the top and looked out, her eyes widened and her stomach dropped. "Charlie. Manuel," she yelled. They tumbled out of the wagon and she pointed toward town.

Over a dozen villagers gathered, armed with torches, pitchforks and scythes. A man in the front shouted, flung his hand in the air, and began to march toward the mission. The rest fell in beside him. She reached for her pistol, then realized she wasn't wearing it. Father Jon had insisted she take it off when she came into the mission. There had been no need for it, he said.

Drawing guns, Charlie and Manuel positioned themselves in front of the gate, waiting.

As if lightning was striking from the gods themselves, horses' hooves thundered in the gathering gloom. The villagers dived out of the way as Brandon charged through them, brandishing his pistol, scattering them left and right. An unsaddled buckskin galloping at Eagle's heels.

Her heart thundering, nearly tumbling in her haste, she raced down the stairs to get her guns.

CHAPTER 18

Twilight.

He'd been in the saddle all day. And all day his skin crawled. His wife was in danger. He knew it. Could sense it. Could taste fear and unease on his tongue. Trouble was brewing.

He rode on. South. Toward the mission.

As the sun began to lower and turn the sullen gray sky purple, it outlined the village ahead, comprised of small adobe homes and a couple of two-story buildings.

He was almost there when he saw it. A gathering crowd of villagers shouting, carrying torches, pitchforks, and scythes, heading for the mission.

Thumping his startled stallion's sides, the horse broke into a run. Brandon urged it faster. Riding low in the saddle, his gun drawn, he reached the villagers and didn't stop. They dived to each side of the street as he rode through them, the buckskin galloping behind.

Hauling on the reins, he brought Eagle to a stiff-legged halt and leaped from the saddle, taking his place beside Charlie and Manuel. The crowd had re-formed and was relentlessly approaching. Gun drawn, he called out, "You folks go home now and I'll pretend you weren't about to murder innocent children."

"Someone who spoke English called out, "They've got smallpox. They'll kill us all."

"I doubt that, but I won't have any problem doing exactly that." The hammer clicked as he cocked it, pointing his Peacemaker toward the crowd.

Charlie did the same.

"Does anyone in town have pox?" Brandon called.

The citizenry shuffled feet and murmured.

"Not yet. But it's just a matter of time. Manuel's mother and sister went in and never came out," a bilingual speaker called out.

"My mother and sister live. No one goes in or out to protect you and yours, Esteban. And the rest of you villagers as well. You, Juan. You, Diago. How many times have the good sisters and father, helped you and yours in your times of need. Too many to count, I would wager." For one of medium stature, Manuel stood tall. Radiating authority. The boy becoming the man, as he continued to name the people in the mob personally.

"And you, Luis. The good sisters saved your wife's life." As he talked, he looked each villager in the eye.

Slowly, with much muttering, pitchforks and scythes were put down. Feet shuffling, the men began to make their way home.

"Brandon."

Blood pumped through his system and a buzzing sounded in his ears at the voice he hadn't heard in two long months. He looked up.

The moon accentuated her as she stood in the

belfry, gun drawn, her glorious mane of hair falling wildly on her shoulders, her amber eyes gleaming like a cat's in the dark. Her red bandana covering the lower portion of her face.

"Lo', O'Malley." His voice huskier than usual as a giant frog leaped around in his throat at sight of her.

"Lo', Wade." Then her head disappeared and he could hear the fast clip-clop of her boots on the wooden stairs.

Long moments later, her breathless voice drifted from the other side of the gate. "You came. I knew you would." Then broke the moment by adding, "What's with the buckskin following you around like a dog?"

"She's not following me. Eagle has made a conquest." He chuckled.

"Like rider. Like horse."

"Open the gate, O'Malley," his voice even huskier than before as an almighty urge to take her in his arms and never let her go flooded through him.

"I can't do that." She heaved a heavy sigh, the words tinged with regret.

"What in hellfire are you talking about? Open this door." His voice went from husky to impatient as his pulse jumped in his wrists.

"I won't expose you to this, Brandon."

"You open this gate or I'll climb over it."

Silence.

Manuel and Charlie looked on with interest.

He was two seconds away from grabbing his lariat and tossing it around the bell pull to heave himself up when the gate creaked and she stepped outside, her hand extended in a stay-back gesture.

His gazed traveled over her hungrily. She was okay. Thinner, and her cat's eyes were rimmed in violet, but okay. Fear for her safety gave way to anger. He clenched and unclenched his fists to keep from shaking her till her teeth rattled. How dare she put herself in danger like this. Ignoring her attempt to keep distance between herself and the three men, he took a step forward, all but breathing fire. "O'Malley, I should —"

Her eyes narrowed but instead of stepping back she stepped forward. "You should what, Wade?"

And there she was, the beautiful, willful woman he'd fell in love with. Bullheaded to a fault and afraid of nothing. "I should kick you out of my bed for a month of Sundays."

She cocked an astonished eyebrow at him. "And who would suffer for that one?"

"Both of us." He yanked her to him, jerked down her bandana and kissed her for all she was worth. When he finally let go, they were both panting. "Good to see you, Red," he managed to get out.

"Kick me out of your bed. You'd never survive the night." She snorted.

"You got that right." And kissed her again.

When Brandon could finally focus on his surroundings, he saw Charlie leaning again the chuck wagon, grinning broadly. Manuel was looking at everything but them, his face brick red.

"Some things never change," Charlie drawled.

"Meez Alex, how is my mother and sister?" Anxiety coated his voice, but he still didn't look at her.

"They're holding their own. No worse. I think they were just so tired and worn down that they succumbed to this awful stuff, but they are getting plenty of rest now. And don't you worry, Manuel. I refuse to let anything happen to them." Her tone fierce with determination. When he finally lifted his gaze to meet hers, she gave a sharp jerk of her chin for emphasis.

"I believe you, Meez Alex. You will save my family."

"Dang right she will, kid," Charlie put in.

"Charlie, are you set on supplies?" Alex asked.

"We are and you're going to have a healthy bill to settle with Manuel's cousin to show for it. Never seen such an accursed—err—accomplished haggler in my life. No offense, kid."

Manuel just grinned.

"I'd better get back in." She took a reluctant step toward the gate. Brandon fell in step with her.

She stopped abruptly, raised a questioning eyebrow then shook her head in denial. "Stay with the men, Brandon. Please."

"Where you go, I go."

She gave him a long look and read the intractable in his face. Then heaved a sigh. "You are so stubborn."

Manuel grinned again. Charlie turned a chuckle into a cough when she shot him a hot look and Brandon said, "Pot and kettle, O'Malley. Pot and kettle."

"So, who's is the pot and who's the kettle?"

"Take your pick," he said as he followed her through the gate. The buckskin tagging behind.

They headed toward the mission stable which

consisted of a shelter with three sides and four stalls. A small donkey in one. Swishing its tail, it wandered out. Brandon looked around with a frown. "Where's Dancer?"

Whether from hearing his name or seeing his beloved mistress, the horse came galloping from behind the mission. Brandon raised a questioning eyebrow.

"Manuel's been gone for several weeks so there was no one to buy oats. Dancer and the donkey have been grazing in the hayfield. And topping off with carrots from Sister Marie's garden. When she finds out about that, she is going to have a fit."

Brandon snorted and dug out the bag of oats, scooped a handful and held it out for Dancer, who nibbled it with the delicacy of his name, snorted in Brandon's hand then head-butted Alex in the chest. She laughed and tugged his forelock.

Brandon took off Eagle's saddle and bridle, and slung them in the makeshift shelter. The stallion and the buckskin meandered to the trough beside a pump and dunked their noses in it.

He turned to his wife. For a moment, he just drank her in. The sight. The scent. The sound.

She met his gaze and smiled.

"You look tired."

"I am, but at the moment I feel whole again. I miss the babies, of course. But having you here..." her voice trailed off.

He took her hands and jiggled them. "I know exactly what you mean, Red." Before Alexandria O'Malley had come barreling into his life, he'd had a full life, a busy thriving ranch, interesting, entertaining women, something always calling over the next horizon. Now, he couldn't imagine a life without her.

"Doesn't mean I didn't wish you would have stayed on the outside of the walls."

"Understood."

"I guess we better get to it." She pulled up her bandana and started to pull up his then dropped her hands. "You better pull up your bandana."

He snorted. "O'Malley, we've already kissed. I don't think you need to be worried about having your hands on me. In fact, I'd welcome it."

"About that," she began.

He saw the worry in her eyes, pulled his bandana over his mouth and nose, and only said, "We'll talk about that later."

She nodded and they strode into the mission. They walked down the long, silent corridor that normally rang with the sound of children's laughter. Now, only the click of their heels sounded against the adobe floor. Rounding a corner, she stopped in front of a room he remembered the sick were housed in. Alex threw open the door and he followed her in.

He thought he was prepared but he wasn't. Flickering candlelight shone down on children from toddler to teen. Most of them with scabby faces and sad eyes. Even with the windows opened to let in the cool night breeze, heat from fever abounded.

Sister Marie looked up from sponging off the toddler and nodded at him. Not questioning, just accepting.

He pointed at a pretty, well-rounded redhead that held the hand of a young boy that stared at her, but didn't seem to see her.

"That's Rosie. She came to collect her nephew and has stayed to help. This horrible disease has blinded him." Horror and pain filled her voice and his heart. The boy looked no more than four or five. Once again, his gaze swept the sick room. Acid spurted in his gut as he thought of Sarah Marie and Jon. Thank goodness, they were safe back at the ranch, far from this deadly disease.

The swishing of a cassock drew his attention from the tragic scene as Father Jon came striding toward them—swirling stale heavy air that should have been arid but wasn't—as he approached.

"I'd shake your hand but the less physical interaction the better. I knew when Alex arrived you wouldn't be far behind. Have you come to take her back?"

He glanced at his wife. "Eventually." Then turned his attention back to the good father. "I'm sorry we aren't meeting under better circumstances. What can I do to help?"

As if too weary to argue, accepting Brandon's decision, Father Jon said, "No one has died in the past week, which is a blessing. We're all taking turns in the sick room, which means the garden, repairs and all outdoor chores have been sadly neglected, perhaps you could see to them."

"Consider it done."

CHAPTER 19

Sundown.

The sun set in a brilliant riot of colors, changing the drab of the adobe walls and mission house to deep purples and bright crimsons. Then the orange ball of light and heat slipped below the horizon, and the walls and building were once again staid earth tones. Matching the mix of reddish, sandy-colored soil Brandon's hoe overturned.

Like their life at the moment, he mused. Radiance slipping into the austere. Vibrant life into sickness and death.

He hadn't visited the sick room after that first time. His wife, Father Jon, Sister Marie and Rosie saw to that.

It ate at him. His wife in constant danger from the contagion while he breathed clean air and was kept away. He could insist, but it would only add to her worry and that was something she didn't need right now.

A whip of sound had him straightening and reaching for his gun.

His hand dropped.

Rosie strode toward the garden, a basket under her

arm. Covered from neck to heels in a plain, serviceable yellow dress. Her riotous red hair hidden under a kerchief. Another at her neck that she was tugging down from her nose and mouth.

He didn't know her well, but what he did know he liked. Like his wife, she had pluck, and he admired that.

She saw him, waved, and headed in his direction.

He shook off the worry, that was always near the surface as long as O'Malley continued to throw herself headfirst in harm's way, and said, "You here for those carrots, you mentioned this morning, you wanted?"

"That and some air that smells of nature and not of sick." She took a deep inhale then yanked up her kerchief.

He did as well then took her basket and began plucking the carrots out of the loosened dirt.

"Here I can do that."

"I've got it." He pulled a few more of the orangey long roots with their multi-topped green shoots, that waved with each tug, then handed her the basket.

"How's your nephew?"

"Brave. My nephew is the bravest little man I've ever encountered. He's not going to let a little thing like blindness slow him down." Her eyes glistened and she bit her lips, then straightened her shoulders and tossed her head.

"He is that. Must take after his aunt."

She threw him a smile that lit up what he could see of her face. "You should have met his momma. There was nothing nor no one she wouldn't take on. By the time I learned she was gone, Bodie had been sent here. And then he caught smallpox. That awful disease took his sight and his best friend here. She was a darlin' little girl."

Her sparkling eyes dulled. Once again she straightened her shoulders. "No one said life was easy." She shook herself and lifted her chin. "Bodie has me now. We'll be just fine."

"It's not and you will. How much longer do you plan to stay? He seems past the contagion point."

"Thank the good Lord. I'm going to stay as long as I'm needed. Until the church sends a replacement for Sister Sarah." She crossed herself. "And I want Bodie to adjust to his blindness in familiar surroundings."

"And then?"

"Eventually, the boy and I are going to Mobeetie. I've an aunt that runs a boarding house there. I'd like to make it there while she's still alive. She's all the kin the boy and I have left. If I can scrape a little coin together, I'm going to open a café. Saloons are a dime a dozen in frontier towns, but cowboys will cough over hard-earned pay for a good home-cooked meal. There may be a lot of things I can't do, but I can cook."

"I'll attest to that." He grinned, studying her. And she could too. She'd taken meager ingredients and turned them into mouthwatering.

She narrowed her eyes and placed her free hand on her hip. "You're looking at me like a chicken that's about to be plucked."

He laughed and shook his head. "I've got a friend by the name of Reuben Hayes. He lives in Mobeetie.

I'd be much obliged if you'd look him up and give him my regards." The two had a lot in common. Tough, no-nonsense and bone deep loyalty to those they cared about.

"If he's still there by the time I get there, I can do that for ye. Though, it won't be anytime soon. May actually be years." Her eyes glanced around, "There's a lot that needs tending to here. And the boy's comfortable."

"Well, once you get settled, get in touch with me. We can furnish you start up money."

"I don't take charity." Her back stiffened and her lips formed a straight line.

"I don't blame you. And it wouldn't be charity. It's a business proposition. A partnership if you will. You're right about cowboys wanting tasty vittles when they're in town. It would be a good venture. Bring me in a little coin. Once you're on your feet, you're always free to buy me out."

Her mouth dropped and she blinked at him. "I don't know what to say."

"Don't say anything. Just reach out when the time comes."

"You're a good man, Brandon Wade." She blinked rapidly and surreptitiously wiped at her eyes.

"Don't let that get out. I don't want my image as a tough hombre ruined," he joked.

"I've heard about that side too. Now I'd better get dinner on the table and food for the young'uns. I'm running right late today." She turned in the gathering gloom and strode away. Disappearing into the shadows.

CHAPTER 20

Storm clouds hovered sullenly, casting dark and gloom on the setting sun.

Clouds that Brandon was pretty sure wouldn't deliver any rain.

Another week had slipped by.

"Boss." Charlie's voice echoed over the gate that Brandon strode toward, as had been his habit every evening since he'd arrived.

"Yeah?" He leaned against the gate and spoke through the knot hole on the side of the door.

"When were you planning to leave for home?"

"You homesick? No pretty senoritas have caught your eye?" Brandon joked, leaning an elbow against the gate.

Charlie snorted. "Plenty. But for some reason they don't seem to want too much to do with us. You'd think we were associated with the plague. So when are we heading home?"

"Soon, I hope. No one has died recently and the children seem to be on the mend. Is there a particular reason you're asking?" Brandon studied his cowhand through the peep hole in the gate. Charlie wore his poker face but there was worry in his eyes.

The villagers cautiously interacted with them now. Especially Manuel's cousin, who was probably set to take over the town as much money as the Silverhills' ranch was pouring into his establishment.

"An hombre that calls himself Thiago is the new leader of the Comancheros. Word is he makes the dead and unlamented Lavarah look like a pussycat."

Thiago. *Supplanter.* Brandon snorted, fighting back the rage that filled him whenever he heard Lavarah's name. Heat built behind his eyes and he fisted his hands. The man that had captured his wife not once but twice and had sold her to her nemesis McCabe then tried to keep her for himself. At least, he was dead. May he rot in hell right beside McCabe.

"Boss?"

"Yeah?" Brandon pulled himself back to the present.

"For the most part, Lavarah stole women. Young, attractive women. Thiago goes after children. He's already hit several villages."

Brandon's heated blood cooled. An icy chill replaced it, filled with foreboding.

"Surely he wouldn't go after the mission with a smallpox epidemic going on."

"How would he know about it? It's not like the Comancheros communicate with the villagers. And the smallpox has been contained inside the mission walls. Chances are no one outside the village is even aware of it. It's a day's ride to the nearest settlement."

"How did you find out about it?"

"A cousin of Manuel's rode in to warn the town

after his village had been attacked. He was severely wounded. Died about an hour ago."

"Damn. I'm right sorry to hear that. Sounds like we're sticking around awhile longer." He was more than ready to be back home. To see his children. Hear the lowing of cattle. Enjoy the bustle of the ranch's community. He'd been gone too long. But he would not—could not—leave these folks while the Comancheros were stirring. He knew his wife would feel the same.

"I thought you'd see it that way."

"Keep a sharp eye out. If you see any signs of trouble fire three shots."

Charlie nodded and spit a wad of tobacco into the sand.

Brandon turned on his heel and strode back toward the mission then stopped as he saw his wife. Attuned to her as to no other, he sensed the tension swirling around her.

"What's wrong?" He came to a stiff halt in front of her, his boots kicking up fine particles of sand and clay.

She shook her head. The bandana moved as her lips parted in a smile that didn't reach her eyes.

"Alexandria." Knowing how stubborn she was, he didn't back off an inch. He hated the violet circles around her eyes, the paste to her skin that high-color and good health normally rode in. Worry lines dug into her forehead. He stared at her uneasily. What could be wrong? The kids were doing better. Had one of the adults come down with smallpox?

He waited. Silent.

Finally, she shrugged. "I was holding the toddler. She's still pretty whiny. Before I realized what she was about she pulled my mask down."

His heart clutched, but all he said was, "I'm sure you put it right back on."

"Not before she coughed on me."

His surroundings blurred. The usual noise of birds and insects came from a long way off. His pulse slowed to where he thought his heart must have stopped then it sped up so fast it was jumping up and down his arms. "Alexandria," he breathed and reached for her.

She jumped back. "No. Don't touch me. Don't come near me."

"Aren't you overreacting?"

"Am I?"

"I'd sure like to think so." He let his hands drop to his sides.

"I'm sorry, Brandon."

He wanted to shake her till her teeth rattled for putting herself in danger, but he pushed down the fury and pulled up the calm. "Not your fault. Let's not buy trouble."

Though he was frightened, and not much frightened him, trouble had already found them. It usually did. But that was life.

"Right." She nodded vigorously, though he could still see the worry in her eyes.

Echoing Charlie, she said, "When are we going home? Everyone seems better, except the little miss who coughed on me. If I do have it, it will break before we reach the ranch. And you leave me, you hear?"

He snorted. "Red, you know I'm not going to do that."

"I know." For a moment, she dropped her head. "What are we going to do? I've been so careful."

"For one thing, we aren't going to buy trouble."

"But—"

"If you do have it, and we're on the trail, we'll send Charlie home and wait it out. Good enough?"

"I'd prefer you to hightail it out with Charlie."

"I'm not good at hightailing. That's the best offer you're gonna get. Take it or leave."

"You haven't given me much choice."

He waited.

"Fine." Then added, "I do love you."

"I know."

"Don't you have something you'd like to say to me?"

"You've had my heart from the first, Red. Even when I was afraid I was lusting after a boy."

She laughed at that. "Were you coming for me or did you need to see Father Jon?"

His mouth thinned. "You. And then Father Jon."

She gave him a searching look. "There's more bad news, isn't there?"

"Could be. Could be nothing. The Comancheros have a new leader. They are raiding villages and stealing children."

"But surely they wouldn't hit the mission when we still have smallpox." Her eyes widened. Her breath quickened, her heart galloping under her blouse. "Unless they didn't know about the smallpox outbreak."

O'Malley had never been slow. She'd gotten to the heart of the matter a whole lot quicker than he had.

"I was going to suggest we leave in a couple of days, but now I'm thinking we'd better stick around. Agreed?"

"Agreed."

"Regardless of Father Jon's disapproval, you need to strap on your six-gun."

She gave a sharp jerk of her chin then strode toward the rundown shed attached to the makeshift horse and donkey shelter where an orange honeysuckle bush bloomed beside it. It's heady fragrance filling the air, diluting the horror of smallpox and the outrage of Comancheros. Calming, she lifted the lid of an old wooden trunk with leather straps that creaked as she opened it, drew out her holster and gun, and fastened it on.

"Let's go see Father Jon." Her shoulders thrown back. Her voice decisive. Steady.

They strode to the sick bay where Father Jon was reading the young ones a story. Even the teenagers were sitting up in bed, listening. There were now empty beds, from youngsters that had fought the disease and won. While the room still smelled of sickness, it didn't have the overpowering thickness that hit you in the face as soon as you walked in that it'd had before.

Father Jon looked up. His gaze zitted to the Peacemaker at Alex's hip and his expression went from one of welcome to frowning concern. "Take over for me, Luke." He handed the book to a nearby teenager and came striding toward them. He'd aged in the short time they'd been there. His hair still thick, but now solidly gray. Worry lines dug into his forehead and while his eyes were almost as bright as they once were, apprehension flickered through them incessantly. Brandon couldn't imagine what it would be like to lose children you'd nurtured as your own. He hoped to never find out.

"What's wrong?"

"Comancheros have been raiding villages, stealing children."

"Children?"

"Children," Brandon said, his voice flat, his lips thin.

Understanding dawned. "And you're afraid they'll hit the mission."

Brandon gave an abrupt nod.

"It would be insanity for them to come here. They wouldn't run the risk of smallpox."

"If they knew about it."

"You're right. The villagers would never mention it. They hate and fear the Comancheros. If they do speak to them, chances are they'll lose their tongues. We could put a sign out, warning them off." Tension radiated from the priest, and something more. Fear. Fear for the children.

"You could. Though, they're so hardened, I doubt if they would believe it. Just think you are using the threat of smallpox as a means to scare them off."

"Then what do we do?" Father Jon's hand slipped to his rosary and he ran his fingers up and down the smooth wooden beads.

"We fight." Brandon whirled on his heel and strode away.

"Where are you going?" Father Jon called to his retreating figure.

"To put rifles in the belfry."

CHAPTER 21

Daybreak.

Leaning on a shovel, Brandon scanned the dozen or so graves lining the back of the mission, partially shaded by the adobe wall and a large weeping willow that the Mexicans called Ahuehuete.

He turned his attention to the small, fresh grave. They'd lost the little girl. She had seemed on the mend, then overnight she was gone. Like the rest of the children, she'd been buried in the sheets she'd died in. A white handkerchief that had been placed over her face after she drew her last breath, along with a handful of other items, sat in a sack next to the grave, waiting to be burned.

Hands incased in leather gloves, he reached for the bag, only to stop with his fingers inches away, as three gunshots sounded in rapid succession.

Jerking upright, he ran for the gate.

"Charlie," he yelled.

"They're coming," Charlie shouted back.

Kicking up fine particles of dust and sand in his wake, Brandon changed direction and charged toward the belfry. Reaching it, he took the stairs two at a time. Old wood groaning under booted heels.

Below him, Manuel and Charlie stood behind

the wagon, rifles raised and pointed south. His gaze tracked in the direction they were facing. Sure enough, riders were approaching, a cloud of dust in their wake. Maybe a dozen or so. He could hear their whoops as they raised their guns in the air and fired them.

The villagers raced for shelter, dragging children by the hand, slamming wooden doors in adobe structures, leaving the streets empty as the hard-riding horde approached.

The steps behind him groaned as someone trotted up them. Rifle in hand, he whirled and saw his wife, chest heaving from the race up the stairs, boots braced on the landing, panting. He lowered his Winchester. She grabbed the other and moved to his side.

The band hurtling toward them was a mix of whites, Mexicans and Comanches. Half of them with bright slashes of war paint on their faces, all with guns drawn. One fired at the handle of the gate, then fell slowly from his saddle as his chest bloomed red. The sound of the shot echoed in the small enclosure, the rifle in Alex's hand smoking. Brandon fired at the rider close behind the fallen hombre and he too dropped from his saddle.

Looking up, the Comancheros saw them and began firing in their direction. Hot lead ricocheted off the bell. The pitted iron clapper swung madly back and forth, amplifying the wild clanging in the small space.

Alexandria dropped to the floor, holding her ears. She kicked Brandon's leg and he hunkered down beside her, covering her body as best he could.

A bullet whizzed through the old wood of the belfry to impale itself on the wall behind them, close enough the heat seared Brandon's face as it passed by.

Pounding heels sounded on the stairs. "Who?" He raised his head and looked at his wife.

"No idea." She crawled toward the opening before he put a hand on her shoulder to halt her then raised his rifle, aimed and waited.

A mass of glinting red hair popped through the opening of the bell chamber. Not the mahogany glory of his wife's, more strawberry and copper. Reinforcements in the form of Rosie O'Leary had arrived. Pistol in hand, she pulled herself up.

"You shoot?" Brandon asked.

She gave him a disgusted look, stood up, aimed and pulled the trigger. A boom sounded followed by a puff of smoke, a scent of sulphur and a desperado fell from the saddle, clutching his shoulder.

Two men fired back.

Brandon pulled her down as hot lead whizzed by.

Alex gave her a sharp, approving nod.

Shots kept coming. Brandon raised up enough to see Charlie and Manuel back-to-back behind the wagon, riders charging from both sides. He fired rapidly. The women jumped up and did the same. Comancheros fell from their saddles, suddenly outnumbered. The original dozen or so now down to two. The one mounted turned tail and whipping his horse up, galloped away in a cloud of dust. The hombre who'd been shot in the shoulder, and fallen, raced for his horse.

"Don't let him get away," Brandon shouted.

Charlie dived at the retreating bandit bringing him down, then clipped him on the jaw for good measure.

Brandon went galloping down the stairs, his blood up, his breathing coming fast and hard. Pulling on his gloves, he raced to the back of the mission, yanked open the flour sack that held the little girl's belongings and grabbed the handkerchief that had lain on her cold still face.

His eyes hot, he strode across the enclosure and threw open the gate. It banged back against stone with a resounding thud. He hauled the marauder up by his shirt front, mashed the small scrap of material in the man's face then shoved it in his pocket. "You give that to Thiago and tell him it's from Brandon Wade, along with the body count of his men. You tell him if he's wants me, I'll be heading for Texas. And I'll be waiting for him." Then he shoved the Comanchero toward his horse. "Now get the hell out of here."

Everyone grew quiet.

"You know they'll come for us," Alex said quietly.

"I'm counting on it. If they're after us, they won't be focused on the mission. Get your things together, Red, we're leaving."

CHAPTER 22

Dawnlight.

The sun broke through the purple and pink sky in an orange swath of glory, holding the promise of a beautiful day. The air clean and clear. Mother nature reflecting Alex's mood.

Dancer threw his head up and down snorting and sidling as if sensing they were heading home. Alex patted his neck, his excitement communicating itself to her or vice versa.

Brandon too was mounted.

Father Jon, Sister Marie, Rosie and Bodie formed a semi-circle around them. The little boy's hand clasped inside his aunt's leaning into her. His blue eyes unseeing. His expression frightened. Alex fought a tightness in her throat that appeared every time she looked at the lad. It wasn't fair for one so young to be dealt such a crushing blow. She bit her lips. Clenching and unclenching her fingers on the reins. Life wasn't fair.

But no matter how heavy the load, his aunt would help him carry it. Her lips relaxed and turned up as her gaze flicked to Rosie. The woman's hair sparkled in the morning sun and her emerald eyes glistened with bright. Alex liked and admired Rosie. She only wished she'd had more time to get to know her.

Brandon reached down and clasped Father Jon's hand. "Appears everyone is on the mend now. And I don't think the Comancheros will be bothering you anymore."

"Yes. I think we are finally through the worst of it. What makes you think the Comancheros won't be back?"

"Because we're leaving." Over his bandana, Brandon's eyes were cold.

"I hope you haven't done anything to put yourself in harm's way, my son."

"Let's just say I've an old score to settle." Of their own accord, his gaze shifted to Alexandria.

A two-fold purpose then in leading the Comancheros away. Well, she wouldn't mind settling with them either considering they had cut out Maria's tongue. She gave him look for look. Retribution in her gaze.

His glance shifted to Rosie and even beneath the red bandana Alex swore she saw his lips turn up. "Don't forget us when you get to Texas. We'd like nothing better than part ownership in that café. Right, O'Malley?"

"Right." It was news to her but she was game.

"Well, there's no hurry about that is there, Bodie?" Rosie glanced down at the little blond head looking at the ground. Alex saw the small hand tighten around his aunt's. He shook his head hard. Once again, her heart clutched.

Brandon turned back to Father Jon. "I left enough money at the supply store that should keep you going for a good long time."

"Not to mention plenty of gold coins in the collection box," Father Jon said dryly.

"Found those did you?" Brandon grinned.

"We will be fine for a long time to come. I can't thank you enough."

"No, Father, it's I that can't thank you. You saved my family. And I will always be grateful."

"Go with God. Both of you." Father Jon made the sign of the cross then stepped back to allow Brandon to turn his horse.

Brandon gave him a two-fingered salute.

"Goodbye," Alex said.

A chorus of goodbyes followed them as they rode through the gate. Hooves clip-clopping and sending up spurts of sand and fine clay. The buckskin trotting at their heels.

"Does she always do that?" Alex turned to look at the mare.

"Yup."

"And I thought you had the ladies eating out of your hand." She shook her head in mock dismay.

"It is rather lowering to be shown up by a horse."

Alex let out a peel of laughter. "Don't you worry. I can attest that your manhood hasn't suffered one iota."

"Glad you think so. Hear that, Eagle," he told the horse. "You've got nothing on me."

They rode up to Charlie, who looked from one pair of laughing eyes to another. "Anything you want to share?"

"Charlie, you should know by now, I don't share. At least where O'Malley is concerned."

"Oh, that kind of conversation." Charlie swung into the saddle.

Heat crept into Alexandria's face, but she threw up her chin to brazen it out.

"Actually, we were talking about Eagle's prowess with the mares."

"Well, he sure has a way with that one." Charlie nodded toward the buckskin, sidling up to Eagle, and gathered his reins.

The saddle creaked as Brandon turned toward Manuel, standing beside the chuckwagon. "You're in charge now."

Manuel nodded, his expression solemn.

"I don't expect you to have any more trouble with the Comancheros, but I have been wrong once or twice in my life."

Alexandria snorted. He ignored it and continued, "You'll get the wagon back to your cousin?"

"I will."

Brandon leaned down and held out his hand. Manuel clasped it. "If you need us, you know where we're at. Or soon will be."

"Godspeed."

Brandon nodded.

"Goodbye, Meez Alex."

"Goodbye, Manuel. Your family is on the mend and will be back with you shortly."

"That is good news." He turned to Charlie. "Goodbye, Charlie."

"Goodbye, Manuel. You're a good man to have on our side."

Manuel gave him a gratified smile.

The three trotted down the dusty street. Villagers stopped to watch. Some offered up waves, knowing the gringos and gringa had saved them. Saved their children. Charlie, Brandon and Alex nodded, then touching heels to their horses galloped out of town.

Once they were on their way, Brandon pulled down his bandana and adjusted it around his neck. Charlie did the same.

Alex left hers in place. Brandon's features tightened. "You feeling okay, Red?"

"Of course. Just being cautious." In a furtive gesture, she crossed her fingers resting on her thigh. Her skin burned and her body ached. But she wasn't about to kick open that particular hornets' nest. She was just tired, she told herself. She would not. Could not. Succumb to smallpox.

CHAPTER 23

Clip-clop. Clip-clop.

Dancer trotted along the trail, tail swishing, head thrown high. Every time one of his huge hooves thumped against the ground pain shot through Alex's back. And she was hot. Hotter than the overhead sun allowed. More like she was frying from the inside out.

More and more she caught concerned looks from Brandon and Charlie.

She ignored them, concentrating on staying in the saddle and not bawling like a babe at the discomfort.

As the day wore on, the landscape blurred. Mist lay over it, but oddly enough didn't block the sun, just the figures riding beside her. Voices came from a long way off.

"We need to stop, Boss."

"We will. As soon as we find a stream or deserted cabin."

Another long period of time passed. Or at least it seemed that way as she swayed in the saddle. The sun getting lower in the sky but the heat from it still burning her skin even through the long-sleeved, faded-blue cotton shirt she wore.

They climbed a rise, dotted with low-growing

scrub grass and an occasional gray-green cardon cactus. Its thorny branches clawing high into the roof of God's country.

Charlie and Brandon reined in. Alex was barely aware that Dancer had halted beside them, along with the buckskin.

"Look, Boss. Down below. There's a stream."

"Ride on ahead and start building a lean-to will you, Charlie?"

"You got it, Boss."

"And, Charlie."

"Yes, Boss."

"When you're done, I want you to head back to Silverhills."

There was no answer. Just the sound of hooves galloping down the hill.

"That's an order," Brandon called after him.

Alex reeled in the saddle. The reins kept slipping from her fingers. She managed to loop them around the pommel then just held on as the horses trotted forward.

Her hands kept opening. In response, Dancer slowed to a walk. Straggly grass cushioning the thud of iron-shod hooves thumping solidly on the ground.

She slipped again. This time a warm, hard hand reached out to push her upright. For a moment she leaned into the security of it, then remembered what she most certainly had and forced herself upright.

"Don't touch."

"Well, that's the first time I've heard that from you." There was a drawl in his voice, but beneath the drawl strain.

"Stay away from me, Brandon. I'm pretty sure I'm coming down with it."

"Not coming down. You already have it. You've got a rash on your face, Red."

"I'd ask you to leave me if there was any point." The words barely a whisper. Once again, she swayed. Once again, he caught her.

"That's downright insulting. You know you'd never leave me."

"In a heartbeat," she breathed out. Hot, she was so hot. And everything ached.

"You never were much of a liar."

"Fooled you though, didn't I?" For a moment, the memory of her dressing up and acting the part of a boy cut through her discomfort and pain.

"So you did." Like rippling water, his voice soothed. In fact, she could smell it. And hear the waves slapping against the bank. She was so thirsty.

The horses stopped. Strong arms lowered her to the ground. Crushed grass cushioned her. Leather groaned as saddles were unclasped. Then she was lifted and lay with her head against the smooth, warm leather.

"Water."

Moments later her head was raised, her bandana pulled down, and her old dented cup held to her lips. She gulped the cool liquid.

"How is she, Boss?" Charlie's voice, distorted and from a distance.

"She's tough. She's going to make it. Aren't you,

Red?"

She wanted to reassure him, but she didn't have the energy. Her back ached and her body burned.

"Red."

She tried to push open her eyes but they were weighted down. Oh God. What if she went blind like little Bodie? A tear escaped her closed lids and leaked out. A warm callused thumb brushed it away.

She heard canvas rustle then a voice, pitched low and next to her ear. "I know you don't like being told what to do, but you fight this. You hear me, O'Malley? That's an order.

"See what's in her backpack will you, Charlie?"

Boots clomped through rustling grass as she drifted off. The voices of her husband and Charlie awakened her.

"What did you find?"

"Some tree bark."

"Probably willow bark. I don't think I can get her to chew it. Ever made tea before?"

"Nope, but can't be that much different than coffee." Again, boot heels stomped away, hitting the occasional rock and rough surface.

Again, she drifted off.

A hard, warm arm wrapped around her shoulders woke her.

"Drink this, O'Malley."

The tin cup was once more placed against her lips, only this time with hot liquid inside it. Barky, bitter liquid.

She coughed, gagged and clenched her mouth

shut.

"Clamp her nose shut, Charlie, and for God sakes, put your gloves on first and pull up your bandana."

She managed to open her eyes to a narrow slit to confirm Brandon was wearing one too. Too bad he didn't take his own advice about gloves. She'd mention that to him when she had a bit more strength.

"Come on, Charlie. Get 'er done. She ain't a gonna bite."

"Not me at least."

"Good point." Brandon snorted.

Before she could protest, fingers encased in smooth leather plugged her nose. Reflexively, she opened her mouth and found hot bark juice running down her throat, choking her. She coughed up half of it, but it just kept coming. She tried to shake her head back and forth but a hand held the back of her neck. She stilled, resigned, and drank the rest of the bitter brew.

Brandon laid her back against the saddle.

"Where you setting up the lean-to?"

"Just a few feet away. Right inside that grove of trees. We'll be concealed among the pine and oak, and the stream is handy."

"Good choice. But it's not we. You're heading back."

"Thought you wanted me to build the lean-to."

"After it's built."

"May be plum dark by then."

"You're as stubborn as my wife." Resignation deepened Brandon's voice.

"Pot and kettle." Charlie snorted.

"Let's get 'er done then."

Grass rustled and twigs cracked as booted heels strode away, the sounds getting fainter as did the pain. It wasn't gone but it was manageable. The sun beat down, but not as harsh. The smell of green mixed with the illusive scent of wildflowers. Alex inhaled and drifted off.

She woke to warm hands wrapped around her and hard arms carrying her. "Where's your gloves?" she mumbled.

"Not to worry. I'm washing my hands."

Her head fell back against Brandon's shoulder and she lapsed into silence. Charlie tossed down her saddle and spread out her blanket inside the lean-to he'd made, which consisted basically of a tarp held up by four poles.

The sun hovered on the horizon. The sky a swath of pink, crimson and purple. A fire snapped and crackled. Orange embers shot up around a blackened pot. A warm breeze carried the scent of cooked rabbit.

While the front and sides of the forest offered them some cover there was still room for the horses to maneuver. Behind them the trees were dense and thick, wide swaths of green and shadow. Barely allowing a man to walk through.

Brandon leaned her up against a rough-barked log, the edge of a knotty hole pressing into her back. She twitched and moved over a couple of inches and promptly began to slide. Brandon stuck out a hand and righted her.

Charlie scooped up a tin cup filled with broth with

meat pieces floating in it. She held out shaky hands and noticed the rash.

"What does my face look like?" she asked.

Charlie and Brandon looked at each other.

"You mean above the bandana?" Brandon asked.

"You're stalling," she muttered.

"By the time we get home, you'll be good as new." Brandon hedged.

"That good." She gave a glum look at her broth.

"The fact that you're even asking tells me the tree bark is working or maybe it's because you aren't bobbing in the saddle. Be a good girl and drink your broth and I'll give you some bark to chew on for dessert."

"Who could turn down an offer like that," she whispered past a raw throat. "Both of you back up." She pulled down her bandana to eat.

As they took a step backwards, she sneezed. They hastily backed up further. She sipped her broth, swallowing past a sore throat. When the cup was empty, she chewed on the willow bark. Exhausted, she sat down the cup. Brandon scooped her up and laid her on her blanket that held the homey smell of Dancer.

"Sweet dreams, Red." At least that's what she thought he said as she tumbled into a dark, dreamless sleep.

~*~

Moments later, or so it seemed, Brandon gave her a quick shake of the shoulder. "We've got company."

She blinked open heavy lids. The sun had set, turning everything a twilight gray. A lightning bolt of pain shot through her head. Ignoring it, she reached for her Peacemaker still strapped to her leg.

"Get behind those oak trees." His voice low, he pointed at two hardwoods that had fused together and presented cover of sorts. She pushed to her feet and wobbled toward the oaks, their deciduous lobed leaves pushing against the neighboring spiky pines. She leaned against them, resting her Peacemaker in the bottom of the V the two trees made. A couple of yards over, Charlie nodded from behind another wide old oak, his Colt in his hand.

Brandon slid behind the pine on the other side of Alexandria. All three motionless.

Over the sound of a hawk screeching overhead, she heard the thunder of horses' hooves. Then men's voices. Harsh. Guttural. Some yelling in Commanche. Some in Spanish. Some in English.

Comancheros.

For one brief moment, Alex panicked. Her mind took her back to a place she didn't want to be. Then she straightened aching shoulders. Brandon had saved her then. They'd save each other now.

"*Negro semental.*" The voice rang out filled with excitement. They'd discovered the horses.

They hadn't hobbled the horses, leaving them free to graze, figuring oats and the stream would keep them near. It usually did. But panicked, they would probably run. The thought had no more formed than the sound of hooves trampling through the underbrush sounded, along with snorts and neighs.

Terror streaked through her, turning her hot body

cold. The chestnut, roan and the buckskin would take off, Dancer wouldn't.

She heard him bellow. Her mind could see him on his hind legs, those mighty front hooves lashing out.

A command in Spanish rang out to capture the stallion. Then the rest of the band was on the move. Closing in. Not even trying for quiet as horses stamped on brush, twigs and crushed grass.

Swaying, Alex started forward.

"Don't even think about it, O'Malley." Brandon's voice low and sharp. "That hoss can take care of himself better than you can."

"I'm not letting them have Dancer." She shoved the words past her aching throat.

"You go out there and I'll have to follow. You'll wind up getting us both killed."

"Damn you, Brandon." Tears threatened to spill over, appalling her. She never cried.

"Damn me all you want, just stay put."

She clutched the entwined trees for support, the dark bark rough. With shaky hands, she once more balanced her Peacemaker in the V of the trees.

A bandolero shouted. They'd found the camp.

"Brandon Wade, I've come for you. Show yourself or are you going to hide like a girl?" A voice rang out.

"Just a little closer, you sap sucker," Brandon murmured, his Colt raised.

"That must be Thiago," Alexandria said hoarsely.

"Yeah," Brandon said.

The leader kept to the trees. One of the men moved to his right.

Brandon fired.

Blood spouted.

Clutching his chest, the man dropped to the ground. His horse neighed, reared then thundered away. Pounding hooves grew faint before disappearing on the wind.

"One down," Brandon murmured.

"How many do you think there are, Boss?" Charlie called in a low voice.

"Can't rightly tell for the underbrush and trees. Even without the brushwood the visibility isn't all that good." It wasn't quite dark, but close enough to make it difficult to see.

An answering volley of gunfire rang out.

"At least a dozen, I'd say," Brandon responded as hot lead caught a branch in the tree he stood behind, snapped it and sent it plummeting to the ground, splintering against his arm in the process, ripping his shirt and leaving a trail of scratch marks on his forearm.

"Circle them."

"Yes, Thiago."

If she'd had any doubts as to whether the leader himself had come after them, she didn't any longer.

As they drew nearer, the Comancheros slid out of their saddles, the trees too dense for the horses to pass through, and began circling around them.

Charlie fired to his right. Underbrush crackled as an hombre fell through it.

Alex couldn't tell if the shadowy figures she saw zig-zagging among the trees was one or three. They tended to fuzz together. She fired at the center and all the figures disappeared. Taking a deep breath, she leaned against the tree to steady herself.

Brandon fired and took out another.

Hot lead flew from the guns of the Comancheros.

A bullet whizzed and a trail of fire burned along Alex's arm. "Well dang." She stared at her arm, not comprehending till blood began to gush. At least it was her left arm and not her shooting arm.

"Dammit, O'Malley," Brandon yelled, his voice panicked.

Her lower lip quivered, which appalled her no end. It was hardly her fault she'd taken a Comanchero bullet.

She glanced in Brandon's general direction.

"Stop the bleeding," he ordered.

His look turned to one of stunned surprise as she aimed her gun in his direction and with a hand that barely wobbled pulled the trigger.

A Mexican in a blue, orange and black serape fell at Brandon's feet, blood spurting through the colorful wrap. Brandon kicked him aside and got back to business.

She turned in the other direction taking out one coming up on Charlie. Charlie returned the favor and wounded one running toward her. Limping away, he now ran in the opposite direction.

The outlaws were falling. A good thing too. She was getting woozy, going in and out of consciousness. Her vision was failing. She hoped to hell she wasn't going blind. Panic raced through her system.

She blinked her eyes then sagged with relief. She could still see. She leaned against the tree and tried to focus.

Brandon fired in rapid succession and dropped three.

A sharp command was shouted in Spanish, and the men turned and ran.

Her horse. She had to see to her horse.

Riders were galloping away as she weaved in the direction of the horses.

"O'Malley." Wade was beside her. She fought him as he tried to stop her.

"Let me see to that arm."

"Dancer."

"Damn you, O'Malley." He guided her toward where the horses had been left.

A bugling whinny sounded.

"That's Dancer." She stumbled forward.

A man lay trampled in the dirt. The stallion galloped toward her, dying light haloing the shiny black coat. Dancer butted her with his Arabian-shaped head, his forelock tickling her chin.

"You're okay," she breathed just before everything went dark.

CHAPTER 24

Strong arms lifted her, calling her out of the black.

"Dang it, O'Malley." The voice continued alternately cursing and cajoling.

"Charlie, wrap something around her arm to stop the bleeding and then we'll take her back to camp. My God, can you believe it? Smallpox and now she's gone and got herself shot."

"I love you too," she managed to breathe out.

And just like that the cursing stop. Warm breath tickled her ear as he said in a low tone, "You scared ten years off my life, O'Malley. Ten years I'd planned to spend with you."

"Ouch." Charlie secured a spare bandana he kept in his vest pocket around her arm, tightening it painfully.

"Sorry, Young Alex. Thought I taught you to duck when bullets come whizzing at you," he teased.

"I must have forgot," she mumbled. "Where's your horses?"

Brandon gave a shrill whistle.

A horse trumpeted and hooves thudded. Eagle came at a gallop, the buckskin behind him.

"Don't expect mine to do that," Charlie said.

"You can ride the buckskin."

"That's good. Cause it's downright embarrassing to have that horse following you around like a puppy."

"She's not following Brandon. Her heart belongs to Eagle," Alex managed to rasp out, trying not to think about the fire burning in her arm and her overall discomfort.

The men gave dutiful chuckles.

They reached the camp, everything now in shadow. The scent of crushed grass rose from earth trampled by over a dozen hooves, teasing her senses, giving a much-needed sense of peace. The camp set like a thumb between the densely populated trees and the grassy verge that ended in the clear stream at its front. The whole surrounded by a few pine that provided protection but not so dense the horses couldn't navigate around them.

Charlie dragged the log back that had been knocked up against a tree by horses' hooves. Brandon leaned her against it and cut her sleeve.

"I'll get some water."

"Thankee, Charlie," Brandon said.

Charlie returned, carrying a fresh canteen of water, his long strides eating up the distance between the stream that rippled and flowed, and the camp, and handed it to Brandon. Brandon held out Alex's arm and poured water over it, cold liquid sloshing on the ground in a stream of reddish-pink. Then he swabbed the wound with a strip of cloth he'd cut from an empty flour sack.

"It's just a graze," he said, his voice coated with relief. He wrapped her arm with another strip from the flour sack.

Charlie sloshed some whiskey into her cup and held it out to her. Her head spinning and her arm aching, she took a slug. The amber liquid burned all the way down. Brandon took a swig from the bottle and handed it back to Charlie, who took a couple of swallows and capped it.

The burning in her throat turned into warmth in her stomach and the outline of shrubs and trees, sharp brown and green in the daytime, took on a misty glow.

"Thank you, Charlie," she whispered.

He raised his chin then dropped it.

"Thanks, Brandon."

"Don't thank me yet, O'Malley. Before this is over, you're going to be cursing me.

"Charlie, saddle the horses."

"Boss, she's lost all kinds of blood. Not to mention it's the next thing to pitch black." Charlie's eyebrows shot up. Surprise on his weathered, shadowed features.

"Better blood than her freedom or more of her blood. They'll be back with a vengeance. We need to put as much distance between them as we can." He looked around as if surprised the sky had darkened into night. "But you're right. I was hoping for at least another hour in the saddle. Wishful thinking on my part. There's not even a moon out. Well then, let's eat and get some sleep. We'll be leaving at first light."

First light was an exaggeration, Alex thought

when he woke her. She looked around seeing nothing but dark.

"How are you feeling, O'Malley?" Brandon squatted beside her.

"Fit as a fiddle," she whispered through a throat that felt like she'd swallowed cut glass. There wasn't a bone or muscle in her body that didn't ache.

Brandon laid a hand on her forehead. "You're running a fever." The words came through tight lips. "I can't tell you how sorry I am to be putting you through this."

"Do what you've got to do," she rasped out.

He dropped a featherlight kiss on the top of her head and pushed to his feet. "I'll take her on my horse."

"Tie me on Dancer." Her voice came out low and husky, but at least she was able to get the words out.

"What?" both said in unison.

"If all three of us are going to make it home in one piece, you two need to keep as much distance from me as you can. Tie me on."

"Red—"

She could tell he meant to argue it, so she cut in, "Please, Brandon. Do this for me." Her head throbbed and she didn't have the will to fight him any longer, all she could do was plead.

Luckily, since she didn't make a habit of it, it was enough.

He studied her, weighing his options, a frown cutting grooves in his brow. "I don't like it."

"Me neither," Charlie said.

"That makes three of us," she rasped out.

He came to a decision. "You heard her, Charlie. Saddle all three horses."

"In that case, you better finish this off." Charlie poured the remainder of the curved, hip-pocket, glass whiskey bottle into her worn tin cup. The handle dented from a careless boot of one of the drovers when she'd first joined the trail drive.

"Thanks, Charlie." Knowing it was the only thing that stood between her and a long, hellish ride, she took it and downed it. This time barely coughing.

In a short period of time they were mounted, the horses moving through green straggly grass and gray scrubs at an easy canter. Tied to the saddle, Alex swayed from side to side. Her hat shading her eyes from the sun, peeping bright on the horizon.

As the day wore on, the effects of the whiskey wore off. Every thump of Dancer's hooves an agony. The rash getting worse. The red dots enlarging and beginning to bubble. Even her hind end hurt. Her head thumped and her arm ached. If she had the energy to reach for her gun, she'd shoot herself. She kept her lips clamped shut to keep from calling for them to stop. Knowing how sick she was, Brandon would have never pushed this pace if he didn't think it was absolutely necessary.

He'd stopped twice to give her a long drink of water and run a wet cloth across her forehead. The liquid lukewarm but compared to the burn in her throat it felt downright cool.

Her head began to nod. She managed to tie the reins around the saddle pommel moments before she fell headlong into oblivion.

CHAPTER 25

Alex's chin drooped on her chest.

"Boss, we gotta stop."

Brandon reined in and studied his wife. The sun, lowering in the west, haloed her still figure, outlined by the blues and purple of the sky. The stifling heat layered a haze on the horizon and blurred her features. He didn't see how she'd managed to last this long. But O'Malley was tough. She'd do what she had to do. The knowledge didn't make him feel one whit better, considering he was responsible for her suffering.

"There's a watering hole about a mile up ahead. We'll make camp there."

Charlie nodded. "I remember passing it on the way to the mission. We stopped long enough to fill up the canteens and let the hosses drink.

"How close do you suppose we are to the cantina? A day? Two?"

"A good day's ride," Brandon answered, his worried gaze still on his wife. They needed supplies. The bark was gone. They didn't have any laudanum and the whiskey wasn't going to hold out much longer. He was counting on Charlie having a backup flask. His was running low.

"Let's get a move on." Brandon straightened his shoulders. Tension running through his body, he gave a light kick to Eagle's sides. The horses loped along, Alex's head and shoulders flopping back and forth.

Twenty minutes later, they arrived at the watering hole, fed by a small stream that meandered down the hill where a rocky dip trapped a pocket of water, the overflow continuing on its journey.

"Want me to throw up a shelter, Boss?" Charlie slid off the buckskin and dropped the reins, allowing the horse to drink from the clear pool.

"Nah. We won't be here that long. Last time, I was hoping we could give Alex a few days to rest. But it doesn't look like that's in the cards."

Brandon leaped off Eagle and strode to his wife where she sat slumped in the saddle. Whether conscious or not was anybody's guess. Grabbing her canteen, he untied her and scooped her out of the saddle, leaning her up against a shoulder-sized gray boulder.

"Drink this, O'Malley." He tugged down her bandana and held the canteen to her lips.

"Any willow bark left?" she whispered.

"Sorry. Most of it got doled out at the mission. I gave you what was left. I'll get you some whiskey." He strode to his saddlebag and pulled out a tin flask that sloshed hollowly. Precious little remained.

Watching him, Charlie asked, "Want me to head on to the cantina, Boss?"

"I'll go. You take care of the horses, build a fire and see if you can rustle up something for her to eat."

"Here, give her some of this." He thrust the flask at

Charlie.

"Better hobble the buckskin." Brandon swung back into the saddle and gathered the reins.

"If I ever find a female that is as fond of me as that mare is of your hoss, I just might think of settling down," Charlie said as he grabbed the mare's reins to keep it from following Eagle.

Brandon laughed then sobered. "Take care of her, Charlie."

"With my life."

Brandon gave a terse nod and put heels to Eagle's warm sides lifting the horse into a gallop. Once away from camp, he pulled down his bandana and took a lungful of crisp air, now cooling as the sun set.

Hooves tossing sand and dust, Eagle galloped hard toward their destination. The sky darkened. Stars came out, large and bright, shadowing spiked-leaved yuca plants, some of them flowering, some taller than his horse.

Reluctantly, he dropped the stallion back to a trot, even that a risk at night. He rode steadily, slowing the horse to a walk when a cloud mass darkened the sky, picking back up to a trot when it moved on, riding through the night.

Brandon urged his tired horse into a canter as dawn broke in spectacular swaths of color, reds and purples and tangerine.

Finally, late in the afternoon, he halted on the flattened rise that overlooked the store and cantina. The two weathered, gray buildings leaning against each other as if to prop the other up.

He put heels to Eagle's flanks and sent the horse galloping down the hill. Brandon reined in close to the store. A loose board, on the old building, creaked back and forth in the stiff breeze. He jumped down and led the horse, blowing and foam-flecked, to the trough, let it drink its fill, then tied it at a hitching rail with a black and a gray. The other three hitching rails full. Horses' tails swished, driving away the giant flies, whose bites left welts. An occasional stomp of a hoof throwing up spurts of fine dust and sand.

He strode into the store. His boot sinking on a worn board.

The old lady, dressed in dusty black, looked up from where she stood behind the equally dusty counter. "You're back." Her voice held more resignation than welcome.

"That's not much of a greeting for a paying customer." He bit back a grin. For all her faults, and he was sure she had plenty, he held a reluctant respect and liking for the old gal. As tough as shoe leather, he had no doubt she'd weathered many a storm.

"Last time you were here, a brawl broke out. I imagine it will happen again."

"Well, until and or if it does, I need supplies."

"You got coin?"

"I wouldn't come in without it."

"What do you need?"

"Same as last time, flour, coffee, oats for the horses, and laudanum or willow bark if you got it."

"Got plenty of willow bark. No laudanum."

"Plenty is what I need. And a couple of bottles of

whiskey."

"You'll have to get that next door. Though you'll probably start a brawl. You better pay me now in case you ain't able afterwards."

Brandon shook his head, thumped down coin then opened the door between the two buildings.

Wood groaned. Hinges shrieked.

Sound ceased as everyone looked up and stared. Scowls creased the faces of those that had been here on his last visit. Curiosity rode on others. Only one seemed truly glad to see him. The young senorita jumped out of the lap she was sitting in and raced to meet him, her elevated heels clicking across the well-worn floor, sending up little spurts of dust. Reaching him, she threw her arms around him.

He gently set her aside.

"Thank you."

"For what?"

"Willer told me what you did."

"Willer? Oh, the old lady."

He strode to the bar with the young woman beside him. Today she wore a dress the color of a dusty rose. The same tight bodice and thin straps as the other. Her makeup just as heavily applied.

"You back?" The barkeep, with muscles just as large as ever, gave him a surly look.

Everyone was certainly glad to see him, he thought ruefully.

"Two bottles of rotgut to go." He tossed down coin.

As the bartender pivoted and reached for the bottles, Brandon turned to the young woman staring up at him with an adoring expression that embarrassed him.

"Why don't you get out of here?" he asked gently.

"Where would I go?"

"If my wife wasn't sick, I'd take you home with me."

"As your—" She didn't finish the sentence just gave him a sultry look.

"Good God no. My wife would kill us both." He literally shuddered.

"Are you afraid of her?" She gave him a challenging look.

"You bet I am. She might put up with a lot from me, but cheating isn't one of them."

"You never cheat on your wife?" She frowned in confusion.

"No."

"Because you're afraid of her?"

He laughed. "There is that but mainly because I love her and I don't need or have a desire for anyone else."

A sad expression flitted over her face then was gone. "She's a very lucky woman."

"I'm the one that's lucky."

The bartender thumped the bottles on the counter.

Brandon tossed down coin, then tossed a double eagle to the young woman. "For room and board."

"Thank you."

"If you ever make it to Texas, there's a spot for you at the Silverhills' Ranch."

"Doing what?" She gave him an intrigued look.

"Cooking. Cleaning. Gardening. Rounding up cattle if you want. Anything except what you're doing now."

"You would take me in?"

"In a heartbeat. So would my wife. Like I said if she wasn't sick, I'd take you with me now, but it would be far more dangerous traveling with us than staying here. What's your name by the way?"

Before she could say more the bandolero whose lap she'd been sitting on grabbed her by the arm and pulled her roughly around. He was middle-aged with a leathery face and wore a blue and black serape. A large sombrero, with a leather chin strap, hung down his back and a scar from his eye to his chin marked the left side of his face. A brawler if Brandon had ever seen one.

"Where are you going, honey? Did you forget you were with me?" Whiskey fumes radiated from his pores and out his mouth.

Brandon had ridden all night. He was tired and not at his best. "Take your hands off her."

"Or what?" The hombre sneered.

"Or I'll rip your arms out of their sockets and beat you with them."

The hombre reached for his gun.

Heat built behind Brandon's eyes. They gleamed with a feral light. People that knew him would have run for cover. Brandon could have outdrawn him, but what was the fun in that? Frustration bubbled and boiled over. The long, hard journey. The Comancheros.

But mainly the fear of losing his wife.

His fist shot out before the hombre saw it coming. It hit between his eyes and downed him like a falling tree. The floor shook when he thumped against it. His eyes rolled back and closed.

Two more men came at Brandon. Another jumped on his back. His blood singing, Brandon lowered his head and charged. He head butted one of the men in the stomach. When the hombre doubled over, he clunked heads with the man riding Brandon. The crack echoing through the saloon. Both men fell to the ground.

The other man stood with his fists clenched, his eyes narrowed. He charged and managed to get in a good hit to Brandon's jaw before Brandon felled him as well.

The rest of the customers came racing toward Brandon.

"Get out of here," he yelled to the young woman. She raced to the store door and disappeared through it.

The bandoleros converged on him.

He threw punches indiscriminately but he was outnumbered. Six or seven to one. He took two hits for every one he got in. The one to the side of his head had him seeing double and his knees buckling but he didn't dare fall. They'd kick the holy tar right out of him if he did, not stopping till they'd killed him then what would become of O'Malley? The thought stiffened his spine and he threw out a haymaker. One of his attackers crumbled. Only five maybe six to go, he thought, his lungs working like bellows as he wheezed air in and out.

He took a hit to the kidneys. Grunting, he kicked out. His boot making contact with someone's crotch. The hombre slowly sank to the floor, moaning.

Four or five left.

Someone threw a punch that landed in his right eye. He could only hope it didn't swell shut before he managed to get the hell out of here.

Bang.

Willer stood in the doorway, rifle smoking.

The fighting stopped. Everyone stood motionless. Brandon wondered if she'd shot him, his body certainly hurt bad enough.

"That's enough. Go on about your business now." She motioned toward the bar. "Mister, grab your bottles then come and get your supplies and ride on."

Grumbling, the men left standing strutted back to their chairs. The men on the floor made no attempt to get up.

Brandon grabbed the two bottles and followed her over.

"Goodbye," a small voice called.

He nodded then followed Willer out of the saloon and into the store. Everything was sacked up in a large flour bag. He added the bottles, picked up the sack and headed for the door.

As he reached it, Willer called after him in a raspy voice, "Your coin is always welcome, but don't be in a hurry to come back. You brawl more than the bandoleros."

He strode out the door, shoved the contents of the sack into his saddlebags and galloped away. Once he topped the rise he reined in.

The sky had darkened, along with one of his eyes, and he couldn't see worth diddly. He let Eagle set his own pace as he headed back the way he'd come, fighting waves of exhaustion that had him weaving in the saddle, threatening to overtake him. It would be a long while before he could rest.

He wondered if his stop at the cantina would help the Comancheros narrow down his location. Then shrugged it off. It wouldn't matter. They had trackers. The best in the country. He turned his attention to the night stars that, along with the moon riding high in a cloudless sky, would help him make his way back to O'Malley.

Ignoring his aching body, Brandon pushed through the night. Hooves clopping. Saddle creaking.

~*~

An hour or so before daybreak, thick dark clouds rolled in, blanketing what little light illumed his trail. Thunder cracked. Lightning speared in a brilliant zig-zag of white light.

Startled, Eagle sidled. Sullen clouds lowered and opened. He calmed his horse as drops plopped on his shoulders and splashed off his hat. Like a snarling tiger, the rain gathered itself and spilled into a downpour. He pulled on his slicker and cursed himself for telling Charlie not to bother with a shelter. Taking a deep breath, he calmed. Charlie would do whatever it took to take care of Alex. To keep her safe.

The rain increased. Now coming down in sheets of wet. A stiff wind pushing it at an angle in his face, while Eagle's hooves threw up cascades of sparkling liquid. Even when dawn broke the sky remained sullen, the clouds dark and low-hanging, dripping with rain.

Eagle clopped on.

It was late morning when Brandon arrived at the, now overflowing, water pool he'd left Alex and Charlie at.

He looked around. Then caught sight of a tarp to his right. A couple of pines directly behind it. Charlie and Alex huddled under it.

A horse trumpeted and the buckskin came galloping toward them.

Eagle's ears twitched and he trotted toward the mare. Reining the stallion in, Brandon climbed out of the saddle, unbuckled it, took off the bridle, grabbed the saddlebags and headed for the tarp.

Alex lay huddled under a blanket. Charlie waited at the edge of the shelter his legs splayed, his hand out.

Brandon dropped his gear inside the shelter and clasped Charlie's hand, peering over his shoulder at his wife. "How is she?"

"About the same. The whiskey's gone and I can't even make her a cup of coffee." He shook his head, his expression mournful.

"Well, there's whiskey in the saddlebags." He gazed at the wet surroundings. "Though, I guess the coffee will have to wait till we get somewhere dry."

"The whiskey will do." Charlie rubbed his hands together, then took a good look at Brandon's face. "Run into a door?"

"Several actually."

"Afraid even that bandana ain't a gonna hide that eye."

"Yeah." Brandon grimaced.

"How do the doors look?"

"A goodly number were stretched out on the floor." With his one good eye, Brandon winked.

Charlie grinned through the bandana.

Brandon pulled his up and strode to his wife. He squatted down and pushed the hair from her forehead avoiding the swelling, blistering bumps.

She opened her eyes, her gaze unfocused and blinked a couple of times as she studied his face. "You stopped at the cantina."

"I can't get anything past you," he teased, lifting her hand and holding it in his leather incased one.

"See what happens when I'm not there to have your back?" Her voice hoarse and raspy.

"You got that right. I gave up trying to get by without you the day I met you."

"The day you met me you thought I was a boy."

"Yes, it was very lowering."

That always brought a smile to her face. This time it ended in a grimace.

"What can I get you, that doesn't require a fire, Red?" He gazed at the steady downpour that drummed on the tarp.

"Did you get any whiskey?"

"I did."

"I'd take that, just don't tell Maria, Martha or Lisa

that I'm starting to drink like a...a...cowboy."

He laughed and stood up. "Don't go anywhere."

"Har-de-har."

Moments later he was back and poured some cloudy amber liquid into her dented tin cup. He helped her sit up then held the cup to her lips. She took a gulp. Her eyes flew open and she started coughing. Finally, the hacking subsided and she gasped out, "That tastes terrible."

"They don't call it coffin varnish for nothing," Charlie said from the corner of the shelter. He leaned back against his saddle, an elbow incased in worn red cotton resting on the ground.

Alexandria made a face then blinked. "It might taste like tar but it cuts right through the discomfort and leaves all my parts numb."

Brandon leaned her back against her saddle. "Go to sleep. We'll leave when the rain lets up."

She lifted her hand to his face then dropped it before it reached its destination. "You do the same. You look terrible. And please don't mention pot and kettle."

"You always look beautiful to me, Red. You know that."

She snorted, closed her eyes and moments later, her breath was deep and even.

"I think I'll take her advice." He strode to his saddle in the opposite corner of Charlie's and dropped to the ground with a groan. The last thing he remembered was the drumming of raindrops on the tarp.

He slept through the day and into the night then

woke briefly. The rain still drummed. Under it he could hear his wife's even breathing. He listened for a few moments then fell back to sleep.

The next time he woke it was to the sleepy chirping of birds. A precursor to dawn. No thrumming of rain broke the birds' chorus. It had finally stopped. Time to move on.

He pushed to his feet and stretched then groaned. Every muscle in his body ached. Every fist that made contact with his body felt. He stepped from under the tarp, the ground squishy and wet. He'd give all his earthly possessions for a good cup of coffee or even a bad one right now. But there wasn't a calf's chance in hell of that. Everything in sight wet.

His gaze pierced the dark, relieved his eye wasn't closed. The trees outlined in black still dripped. By the time he got the horses saddled, dawn should be breaking, lightening the sky. They needed to be moving. The only consolation, the rain would have slowed down the Comancheros and it had given Alex a chance to rest.

His boots squishing, he slogged through the wet. After seeing to his own needs, he saddled Eagle then gave all three horses a meager handful of oats. When he returned to the shelter, Charlie was up, his saddle over his shoulder, heading for the buckskin. They nodded in passing.

Brandon grabbed his canteen, some hardtack and willow bark from his saddlebags, then woke Alex.

"Is there anyone in the cantina you didn't fight?" She examined his face, her voice raspy, her rash pronounced and puffy.

"The girl, the old woman and the bartender." He gave her an easy grin.

"Good thing on the bartender. Pretty sure you could have taken the girl. Not so sure about the ole lady. She's feisty."

"Anyway you meant that, I believe I've been insulted." He arched an eyebrow.

"Okay, I'll give you the old woman, but I know you and pretty women."

"You knew me and pretty women. Besides, that's when I thought you were a boy. And even if I had any desire to stray. Which I don't," he added hastily. "There's no doubt you'd geld me. A prime reason to stay faithful."

She snorted.

He turned serious. "That girl shouldn't be there. She can't be more than sixteen."

"So, what do we do about it?"

And there she was. His woman. A gun in one hand. Justice in the other. And never walking away from trouble when someone was in need.

"Unless you want to expose her to smallpox, nothing to do about it this trip."

Charlie, who'd been listening unabashedly, chimed in, "If'n you want, when this trip is over, I could go back for her and bring her to the ranch."

Alex's eyes filled and leaked over.

"Here now, don't do that. It was just a thought, forget I even said it."

"I love you, Charlie," she sniffled.

"And we'll all forget you said that." He threw Brandon an uneasy look.

"Like a brother," she added, with a watery chuckle. "I think it's a wonderful idea."

"There's nothing saying she'll come," warned Brandon, though he felt lighter. It didn't set well leaving a child in the next thing to a brothel.

"It will be her decision, won't it? Anyone want some jerky?"

"I'd kill for coffee," Alex muttered.

"You and me both, Red."

"Well, it's a good thing I threw a tarp over the handful of twigs I managed to collect now, ain't it? They'll smoke some but they should light. Just couldn't very well start a fire in the downpour last night nor under the tarp."

"Charlie, if I didn't have smallpox, I'd kiss you," Alex rasped out.

"You need to stop talking like that." Charlie took a spry step away from Brandon.

Brandon only grinned. "She's got the right of it, Charlie. I might kiss you myself."

"I don't think so." Charlie looked more alarmed than ever.

Alex chuckled and Brandon laughed out right, then said, "Get that fire a going."

Brandon tore down the tarp while Charlie got a small fire, that tended to smoke, going. The wind blowing the acrid black fumes directly at them. But the coffee was worth it. They sat drinking it as the dawn broke. Rosy red and tangerine replacing grey and dark. Alex dunked her hardtack in the strong brew that contained a healthy dollop of whiskey. The whiskey and wet biscuit easy to swallow on her sore throat.

As she set her tin cup down, Brandon handed her a piece of willow bark.

"I don't need it."

He studied her. The bumps were definitely visible, but her eyes were clearer than they'd been in a while.

"For later then, in case you change your mind on the trail." He stuffed a piece of bark into her vest pocket.

"I don't know if I could swallow it."

"If you need it, just nibble on it and if that doesn't work there's always whiskey."

"I'm going to be a drunken sot by the time we get back."

"Not to worry. I won't let that happen, now let's be on our way."

He saddled Dancer and tossed her on.

"I can mount on my own," she rasped out gathering the reins.

"Of course, you can," he soothed.

She scowled at him but didn't say anything more.

As the blue pushed the red out of the sky, leaving only the warm bright orange of the sun, they headed north. Always north. Towards home.

Even with the sun out, the ground remained squishy and damp, as if they were on the heels of the downpour, following in its wake.

"I keep thinking we'll ride out of the wet, but

that storm must have encompassed miles," Brandon remarked.

It was late afternoon when they heard the roar of rushing water. They exchanged uneasy glances as they headed their horses towards an arroyo that they normally rode through. They reached a rise and looked down in dismay. Like liquid thunder, water snarled along the canyon floors, climbing its walls and flooding its rocky surroundings.

CHAPTER 26

Searing sunlight beat down. The arid air diluting its intensity. Waves slapped against rocks as swelling water rushed through the arroyo below. The arroyo they needed to cross to get home.

Exhausted, Alex swayed in the saddle. With shaking hands, she took a sip of the tepid water in her canteen, cooling her parched throat, before carefully stoppering the container.

"What now?" she managed to croak out, trying to straighten her shoulders so Brandon and Charlie wouldn't realize how exhausted she was. She managed for a couple of heartbeats then as if they had a will of their own, her shoulders slumped, again.

"We either wait for the Comancheros or climb till we find another trail." Brandon's eyes hard, his voice grim.

Given the choice, Alex would prefer waiting for the Comancheros but she managed to keep that little nugget to herself. These two men, her husband and her friend, were risking everything for her. The least she could do was hang on.

Charlie looked at the low hanging sun glinting on the mountains, turning them from a dull reddish-brown to gold. "You ain't planning on climbing in the dark." It was a statement, not a question.

"Nope. But we need to head up the mountain to find a place to camp. I don't want the Comancheros taking us by surprise with nothing but a flooded arroyo at our backs."

By unspoken consent, Brandon took the lead and Charlie the end. Alex sandwiched safely between them.

Seeing no trail, Brandon urged Eagle upward, his mighty hooves looking for purchase, throwing rocks and pebbles behind him, the still damp clay giving the big stallion traction as his hooves dug into it, leaving his hoof prints behind.

Dancer followed next, his hooves larger but his steps delicate. Mighty tendons bunched and quivered as he loped up the mountainside as agile as a goat.

The buckskin stood at the base, wanting no part of it.

"Dad-blamed horse." Charlie's voice carried on a stiff breeze.

The buckskin bugled in distress.

Eagle whinnied.

The mare trumpeted and clattered straight up the mountain. Hard, skittering hooves causing pebbles and rocks to bounce down the slope.

Taking a quick look over his shoulder, Brandon grinned. "You could take some lessons from that mare, O'Malley."

She narrowed her bloodshot eyes, but didn't have enough breath to correct him. Then saw him wink, just shook her head and hung on.

Neigh. The sound high-pitched and frightened came from behind her.

Alex whipped around in her saddle, causing her muscles to protest, sending shards of pain from her head to her toes. Then all thoughts of discomfort vanished as she watched in terrified alarm, her pulse racing, her heart thumping.

The mare was sliding downhill. A foot. Two feet.

Then with a stiff-legged, grinding halt, the buckskin managed to right itself. The horse stood trembling, the whites of its eyes gleaming in the dusky gloom.

Charlie tapped the mare with his heels but the buckskin refused to budge. Grumbling and cursing, he vaulted out of the saddle and nearly took a header down the hillside.

Alex gasped.

"Be careful," Brandon called, his voice sharp.

"Boss, you need to find some sort of a trail that is horizontal, instead of straight up, pretty darn quick," Charlie called out, his tanned face white beneath his hat.

"Looks like it levels off a bit just up ahead. We'll see how far it takes us. And if that hoss starts to fall let go of the reins. Don't go sailing down with it."

"Count on it."

Brandon nudged Eagle forward, rocking in the saddle to the horse's uphill gait, Dancer on Eagle's heels.

Alex kept turning in the saddle, oblivious to the

discomfort coursing through her.

Charlie gave a sharp whistle. "Come on, hoss."

The buckskin's ears twitched. When it saw Eagle moving upward, it leaped forward, sending Charlie scrambling with it. One hand on the reins, the other clawing into the dirt and soil, along with his boot heels.

Ears flattened, the mare butted into Dancer, who lashed out with his back heels and began to slide.

"Untie yourself," Brandon yelled, his voice hoarse with fear. Alex scrambled to obey, while Dancer slipped and slid, knocking the buckskin to the side. The big horse righted itself and, with hooves ringing, went tearing up the mountainside, leaving the other horses behind. Alex clinging like a leech. Reaching a rocky ridge, Dancer came to a stiff-legged halt.

Alex looked down and let her breath out in a whish of relief when she saw that no one had fallen. Both horses were moving steadily upward, the mare settled now that it was directly behind Eagle.

Pebbles tumbling, Eagle landed on the ridge, crowding Dancer, who snorted and took a few steps forward around the curve of the mountain. Moments later, the buckskin scrambled up, trembling and blowing. Charlie cursing.

"Look." Alex pointed.

A trail curved downward, winding its way northward, well above the raging water.

Her pounding heart slowed, along with the hot blood zitting through her system. Danger over. Everyone now safe. Of a sudden, tiredness set back in, pushing down on her.

"You did it, O'Malley. You found a passable trail over the arroyo." The voice came from a long way off. She swayed in the saddle. Her eyes closed.

"O'Malley? O'Malley!"

CHAPTER 27

Brandon caught her as she teetered in the saddle. She'd always been nothing but bone, muscle and heart. Now those bones were protruding and sharp, the muscles softening. Even through her bandana her cheekbones looked like they could cut parchment.

"Charlie, why don't you see if there's a spot up ahead to make camp. If not, we'll get 'er done here." Here being a narrow rock ledge that if you rolled over in your sleep you might go bouncing down the side of the mountain to the gushing water below.

His cowhand gave a short chin-dip and trotted the buckskin around the curve of the mountain.

"Put me down, Wade." Her voice labored, Alex didn't open her eyes.

"Not a chance. I enjoy the feel of you in my arms."

Amber gleamed as she opened them a slit.

"I've got smallpox, you shouldn't be this close to me."

"I'd hold onto you, Red, if you had leprosy."

She gave a snort that turned into a coughing fit. His grip tightened, right along with his heart. Finally, she rasped out, "Please, Brandon."

"Alright, but don't go rolling off." He squatted,

leaning her against the rocky slope of the mountain. "Eat some of your willow bark." He reached in her vest pocket.

"I'm not up for that sort of thing," she said as his fingers brushed her breast.

"More's the pity. Though, I'd hate to take a tumble into all that water while rollicking with you, so maybe it's just as well."

That earned him a small smile.

Brandon heard the clip-clop of hooves as Charlie rounded the bend.

"There's a spot up ahead, Boss."

"Then let's go." He picked up Alexandria and placed her back on Dancer. "Do I need to tie you?"

She shook her head.

He frowned chewing on that one. The last thing she needed was to go bouncing down the mountain-side. He wrapped the rope around her waist.

"Why did you even ask?" She heaved an exasperated sigh.

"Beats me. It's loose." He turned his attention to Charlie. "How do you intend to get turned around?"

"Carefully. Very carefully." Charlie climbed down. Standing at the edge of the narrow trail, he threw the stirrup over the saddle and managed to turn the buckskin. The mare's shoulder still scraped against the edge. Snorting, the whites of eyes showing, the buckskin tossed a well-shaped head up and down, but didn't sidle.

"Let's go." Brandon waited till the buckskin and Dancer were on the move then nudged Eagle forward.

The horses clopped along the narrow path. It wasn't as bad as the Narrow Divide, but it wasn't a whole heck of a lot better either to Brandon's way of thinking.

"How much further?" Brandon asked.

"A quarter of mile most."

Brandon grunted. His mouth tightened as he watched his wife sway in the saddle. "Just a bit further, O'Malley, then you can rest."

He thought she nodded but he wouldn't have sworn to it.

Hooves clattered against rock.

A white mountain goat came leaping down the mountain straight at them, sending small stones bouncing their way. The two stallions threw their heads up and down, snorting, their sides quivering but remained stoic. Not the mare. Whinnying and dancing backwards, the buckskin skittered from side to side.

"Charlie, get that dang mare under control before you take a dive a long way down." Charlie tightened the reins and brought the mare to a stiff-legged, trembling halt.

The goat, almost upon them, did a sharp turn and went leaping back up the mountain.

Nerves jangling, Brandon eased his horse forward. He swayed in the saddle to Eagle's rhythm as the worn trail, strewn with dust and pebbles, wound downward.

And then, there it was.

CHAPTER 28

An opening yawned dark and wide to his right.

He moved past Charlie and Alex, turned Eagle into it and hollered over his shoulder, "You found a cave."

"*Cave. Cave. Cave,*" echoed through the chamber.

"It's not very deep," Charlie called back.

"Doesn't need to be." The saddle creaked as he swung out of it, untied Alex and lifted her down. Striding in, he leaned her against a cool cavern wall. The light from outside puddling near the entry, reflecting and shimmering on a small pool inside the cave formed when rain dripped through tiny fissures in the porous rock.

She slipped downward, nearly banging her head on the stone floor. He tugged her back up.

Charlie led the horses to the pool, took off their saddles and gave them a meager portion of oats. Brandon picked up debris, started a small fire and made coffee then passed around hardtack and jerky. Alexandria didn't eat the jerky but she dunked her biscuit in the coffee Brandon had liberally laced with whiskey. It wasn't long till she was leaning back against her saddle, snoring softly.

"How's she doing?" Charlie asked, his voice low.

"As well as can be expected, tied onto a saddle all day instead of resting in a bed." Brandon took off his hat, ran restless fingers through his hair then shoved it back on.

He reached for his coffee, while Charlie chewed on his jerky, took a swallow then said, "I didn't have any choice. I had to get the Comancheros away from the orphans." It was the same thing he'd told himself a hundred times since they'd left the mission, but it didn't stop the bone-deep guilt that ate at him. What if something happened to her because he'd insisted they leave the mission? His hands tightened on the tin cup till the cup gave. He relaxed his grip.

"She wouldn't have it any other way, Boss."

"Yeah, I know." He heaved a sigh and took a gulp of his coffee, wondering where Willer got her coffee beans. Unlike the rotgut they sold at the cantina, the coffee wasn't half bad. The rotgut they probably made themselves.

He tossed down the rest of his coffee, dropped onto his blanket and was asleep before his head hit the saddle.

~*~

With the dawn came crisis.

Alex's rash had turned into pustules filled with fluid. Her fever high.

Charlie built a fire from animal bones and debris then made bark tea for Alex, liberally dosed with whiskey. She drank it down, not having the energy to fight or complain, before falling back into an uneasy sleep.

"Charlie, I want you to head back to the ranch." Brandon glanced at his wife. "It was different when we were in the open, but we're in a more contained area now." He glanced at the dank, dark walls of the cave. "Your risk is greater. She'd want you safe and clear of this thing."

Charlie snorted. "Of course, she would. That's how she's made. You're not leaving her. Don't expect me too."

"She's my wife, Charlie."

"And she's my friend."

"Don't make me fire you."

Charlie clamped his lips together but gave him look for look.

Brandon considered himself a fairly smart man. Smart enough to know that throwing himself against an immovable object would only damage his shoulders. He'd told Charlie to head back once before and been ignored. This time would be no different.

"Have it your way. Probably, just as well. Without me to keep you out of trouble you'd probably just stumble into the Comancheros."

Charlie's lips twitched but all he said was, "Sounds like I better stay put."

The day progressed and rolled into another. Alex's fever continued to climb. The blisters filled and leaked. She weakened.

Brandon now had to force small bites of hardtack soaked in willow bark tea and whiskey down her throat.

Fear and tension drifted through the cave like wisps of smoke from the smoldering fire. On the third night, a thick mist rolled in blotting out the stars, leaving the heavens hidden and sullen, as if waiting. Along with the mist, dread leached into his pores and he couldn't seem to shake it. "Don't you even think about dying on me, O'Malley," he whispered in a harsh voice as Charlie slept and the sky lowered. Exhaustion that he'd managed to keep at bay hit him like a boulder. He lay down beside his wife and held her hand. Overwhelmed by fear and fatigue, sleep crashed down.

"Brandon?"

Light poured through the cave's opening and the occasional chirp of a bird could be heard outside.

Brandon blinked, trying to throw off the heaviness of exhaustion.

"Brandon?" The voice came again.

He rolled over and looked into amber eyes, cat's eyes, completely lucid, with no film covering them.

"Why are you this close and holding my hand? Are you sick?" Panic filled her voice. A voice that was raspy but more than the whisper it had been.

"How do you feel?"

"Weak, but better. My back is no longer throbbing and my throat's not sore. What about you? Why are laying so close? Have you come down with it too?" Her eyes, above the bandana, were worried.

"I thought—Never mind it doesn't matter."

"You thought what?"

He cleared his throat, his voice low. "I thought I

was going to lose you."

"So, you put yourself in harm's way and took the chance of dying with me? What were you thinking? Don't answer that, you obviously weren't. Now move away from me."

His heart, that had been cold and heavy, lightened. She was going to be okay.

She tugged at his hand. For a moment, he held on, his grip tightening. Reluctantly, he let go and pushed to his feet.

"Think you can eat something?"

"I could eat a whole buffalo right now."

Behind his bandana, he grinned.

"Well, I haven't seen any buffalo on this mountain and unless a mountain goat comes leaping by, you're going to have to settle for hardtack and jerky."

"I'll take it and if it's all the same with you, I'd rather have some coffee than anymore tree-bark tea." Even with her bandana on, he could see the grimace and hear the glum in her voice. O'Malley was on the mend.

Charlie strode over, bearing a tin plate with jerky and hardtack and a tin cup that steam rose from, bringing with it the strong rich scent of coffee.

Alex pushed up, leaned back against the saddle and held out her hands.

"Thanks, Charlie."

"Glad to see you're better. You had your husband worried."

"Good thing you took everything in stride." She took the plate and cup.

"Somebody has to keep their head." He winked at her.

Behind the bandana, her lips turned up as she sat down her plate and made a shooing motion. "You two back up so I can pull down this bandana and drink this fine-smelling coffee."

Neither bothered to point out they'd been around her with her mask off when she was too weak to feed herself.

She took a healthy gulp and came up coughing. "You doctored it," she whispered once the coughing had subsided.

"I'll be happy to add a bit to my own brew if it will make you feel any better." Again, Charlie winked then stomped on a spark that a brisk wind had blown near his boot.

Alex gave a rusty chuckle.

Charlie poured two cups and filled two plates with hardtack and jerky, and handed one to Brandon who'd strode to the fire and pulled down his mask.

"Charlie, when you finish—"

"That was my plan." Charlie interrupted Brandon.

"What was your plan?" Brandon's eyebrows shot up.

"Ride down the trail, see if the water has receded and if there's any sign of the Comancheros."

"Then what are you waiting for?" Hands on hips, Brandon's gaze drilled his cowhand.

"Nothing, I guess." His eyes twinkling, Charlie wolfed down his breakfast, tossed the rest of his coffee on the ground, saddled the buckskin and rode out.

He was back sooner than expected.

Charlie pulled up his mask and swung out of the saddle. "Water's down. We can cross the arroyo."

Even in the gloom of the cave, Brandon could see the worry in his cowpuncher's eyes. "Comancheros?"

"They must have found a different way around. They're waiting for us all right."

Brandon swore then came to a decision. "We'll have to travel at night or we'll be picked off like prairie dogs."

"At night? Down that trail?"

"It's either that or wait them out. The horses haven't had anything but a few handfuls of grain in several days. And our hardtack and jerky are getting low. I don't think Thiago is going anywhere. He has an image to maintain and I tarnished it when I sent that contaminated handkerchief."

"Well, I will say, Boss, when you piss someone off, they stay pissed off." He spit a stream of tobacco juice that splat on gray pebbles. "Though, I gotta admit, that was a nice touch. Too bad the bastard didn't catch anything from it. Pardon my language." He nodded at Alex.

"You aren't saying anything I wasn't thinking," Alex responded.

"We would have the element of surprise." Charlie rubbed his chin. The sound of raspy whiskers only slightly muted by the bandana. "No sane person is going down the mountainside at night."

"There ya go. Tonight then?"

"Tonight."

CHAPTER 29

Stars sparkling bright as diamonds lit an ebony sky. A full moon illumed the rough trail they traveled. Brandon glanced back to see Alex swaying to Dancer's rhythm and the clip-clop of his hooves, her eyes closed. And even though the pustules were all over her and she was weak and tired, he'd like to think she was a little better.

His skin tightened and his lips formed a thin, straight line. And if she wasn't, what was he doing to her? Acid spurted in his gut. How much more could she stand? How much more must she endure? He forced his white-knuckled grip on the reins to loosen and his shoulders to stop twitching. O'Malley would endure whatever she had to. She might come in a pretty package, but she had grit. Bottom. Courage. She wouldn't give up and she sure as hades wasn't going to die on him. He'd make sure of that. He straightened, once more riding tall in the saddle, and turned his attention back to the trail.

They rode in silence. The horses at a walk. The trail arcing down. Pebbles rolling under hooves and bouncing down the trail, always inches away from disaster.

As they rounded a curve, Brandon reined in. He held up a hand then pointed down. Below, a camp-fire burned bright. Embers shot toward the heavens, orange against the ebony night. Muffled voices carried in the stillness.

"Now, we wait," Brandon said in a low voice.

Time passed. An hour. Then two. Charlie reined in the buckskin as it tried to sidle up to Eagle, kicking a large rock off the side of the mountain that went tumbling down, bouncing against the canyon walls with a loud clack.

Brandon stiffened and put his hand on his gun.

No one in camp paid any attention. With a whoosh of pent-up breath, his hand dropped from his gun. He threw Charlie a speaking look. His cowhand shrugged. Brandon could almost hear his thoughts. "What can I say, the hoss is in love." The idea had a smile tugging at the corners of his mouth.

Finally, the camp grew quiet. Brandon motioned them forward.

Their horses clip-clopped down the narrow, windy trail. Slowly. Carefully. Their shadows riding beside them on the mountainside, lending an eeriness to the night. The only sounds, the whisper of the wind, an occasional loosened pebble and the scurry of small rodents. A great-horned owl, its wings flapping against the breeze, flew down under Eagle's nose, scooped up a mouse and disappeared into the night.

Eagle snorted, but didn't sidle.

At the mountain's base, the fire burned low, embers glowing against the black. The sound of voices died. The Comancheros stretched out in slumber across the end of the arroyo.

Brandon's gaze searched the camp but he couldn't see a sentry. They apparently didn't feel two men and a woman offered much of a threat. He was torn between relief and disgust. To his right he heard the snort and stomp of horses.

If someone woke and heard them, hopefully they'd think it was their mounts, tied to a line rope between two trees. He pointed to their right and headed for the horses. He motioned for Alex to keep going. She gave him a questioning look but, for a wonder, obeyed. He waited for Charlie and pointed at Alex. Charlie nodded his understanding. As soon as they had disappeared into the dark, Brandon slid from the saddle and began cutting the ropes that bound the horses to the rope-line. The horses began to nicker and stomp and wander away.

He had two left to go when someone yelled, "Hey." Followed by a shot that rang loud in the night.

Swiftly, he cut their ropes then vaulted into the saddle.

"Heeya." He rode straight down the middle of the startled horses that hadn't already meandered away. Clapping heels to Eagle, riding low in the saddle, he tore off into the night, the horses thundering around him.

Men were shouting and firing indiscriminately.

A horse screamed.

"Don't shoot the horses, idiotas." Brandon recognized, Thiago's voice.

On flat ground, the horses continued to run, stretching out long legs. Spooked. Scattering. Ahead of him, the buckskin Charlie rode stumbled then jerked upright and continued on, limping heavily. Brandon reached out and grabbed the halter of a piebald as Eagle and the painted horse hurtled forward, side by side.

The sounds of the Comancheros faded. The horses continued to gallop. Charlie slowed the mare to a trot. Brandon caught up with him. "That buckskin alright?"

"She's limping pretty bad."

"Want to switch mounts?"

"Yeah, think I'd better."

Alex slowed too.

"You doing okay?" Brandon asked his wife. The moonlight lit her features, white beneath the scabs.

She nodded. "You?"

"I'm fine."

They reined in and Charlie switched out horses then climbed back into the saddle.

"Let's get in another mile then stop for the night, if we can find a spot of grass, and let the horses feed. They won't be able to round up their mounts before morning. That should buy us some time. But tomorrow we're going to have to ride like the devil is on our tail, because he will be."

CHAPTER 30

Rushing blood, keeping her going through the mad scramble to escape, slowed. Clogged. Weakening her to the point of nausea. Her body burned and her stomach rolled. She forced aching shoulders to straighten, trying to hide her fatigue, not wanting to slow them down.

Brandon gave her a searching look and drew his own conclusions. "Hang on just a little bit longer, Red. Then you can get some rest." Nudging Eagle with his heels, he started forward. Alex and Charlie falling in behind. The limping buckskin bringing up the rear.

Her headaches and backaches were back with a vengeance. She wrapped the reins around the saddle pommel and held on, trusting Dancer. Her eyes closed. The rhythm of the horses' hooves thudding against clay and sand lulling her. She wasn't certain how long they'd traveled before the thudding turned to a swishing as the horses trod through long, narrow leaves of grass. And still they stayed on the move. Each hoof clop, no matter how gentle, jolting her spine and spearing her head.

Finally, when she thought she couldn't go on, they stopped.

Strong arms lifted her out of the saddle.

"It's okay. You can rest now, O'Malley." She was asleep before Brandon laid her on the ground, barely surfacing when he thumped down her saddle and blanket and shifted her onto it.

She slept like the dead.

The chirp of birds and the lighting of the sky nudged her consciousness, just as the nutty scent of fresh coffee and cooking oats teased her senses. She pushed up on her elbows, and while tired as the devil, her headache was gone.

"Oatmeal?" she asked hopefully.

Brandon poured dark, fragrant liquid from a granite coffee pot into her mug then ladled a dollop of oatmeal from a small cast-iron skillet onto a tin plate and brought them over. "I figured since the horses had grass to graze on, they could share some oats." He winked at her.

She pulled herself up, reached for the warm plate and cup then waited till her husband backed up to pull down her bandana. She took a large gulp of coffee and coughed. She should have realized it would be doctored. Setting down the coffee, she started shoveling in the oats he'd laced liberally with sugar. "Good," she mumbled around a mouthful.

He winked at her then went and got his own.

Charlie woke up and wandered into the underbrush. When he came out, he helped himself to breakfast.

"How's the buckskin?" Alex asked.

"She's strained a tendon. She'll be okay. Especially

since she's not being ridden. It would take more than that to keep her from Eagle." He grinned then asked Brandon between scoops of oatmeal, "How far are we going to try to get today?"

"I'd like to get to the Narrow Divide."

"That's a healthy ride."

"It is that. But it puts us one step closer to the Rio and that puts us one step closer to home.

"You up for it, Red?"

"Yes. Yes, I am." The sleep had done her all kinds of good. As did the oats she was eating. Her appetite had come back with a vengeance. She looked down at her scabby hands. Now if she could just get her skin healed. She couldn't go back to Silverhills till every single pustule was gone.

"Want more?"

"I believe I do."

Brandon gave her a pleased grin and pushed to his feet.

She shoved the plate away from her so he wouldn't come too near when he filled it and inched it back after he'd scraped the remains from the pot into it. She gulped it down in three good-sized bites before raising her cup to finish her coffee. Sunlight glinted off silvered-tin as the sun burst over the horizon in a glow of uneven tangerine and pink strips, making her squint.

Finishing her coffee, she headed into the underbrush. When she came back, the horses were saddled and the fire put out. She swung into the saddle, the ache in her back more of an annoyance than an actual pain.

They headed out, riding hard for most of the day. The buckskin limping behind them. Sometimes out of sight, but always catching up.

Alex's back was once again throbbing, the pain clenching her muscles, but she kept it to herself. She wanted to get as far from the Comancheros as they could. Would the bandoleros follow them to Silverhills? Unease skittered up and down her spine, causing nerves to bunch and jump, remembering when Lavarah had raided the ranch, kidnapped her and killed Joe. There wasn't a day went by she didn't mourn him.

Shaking off her unease and grief, she concentrated on staying upright in the saddle.

They arrived at the Narrow Divide in late afternoon. The sun beating down on weary shoulders. Perspiration beading overheated pores.

A giant, waxy-surfaced saguaro cactus, at least forty feet tall, sat in solitary splendor on the left of the gully among rock and spindly sage, stretching its columnar arms toward the sky.

The buckskin came limping in, just as a mountain lion screamed overhead, causing the horses to skitter. The riders craned their necks, trying to catch a glimpse of the cat.

"Think that's your cat, Young Alex?" Charlie took off his hat, scratched his head, then shoved it back on. "Did she tell you she saved a mountain cat?" Charlie asked Brandon.

Alex was making faces and shaking her head, trying to catch Charlie's attention.

Brandon turned and gave her a long look. "And just how did you do that, Red?"

"She freed its paw from the rocks."

"You freed its paw from the rocks," he repeated, his eyebrows arched, then turned to Charlie, "And you let her?"

"Seriously, Brandon?" She gave an unladylike snort. "Nobody, including you, let's me do anything," she managed to say over the thumping that had started back up in her head.

"Point taken. I know you have an affinity for animals and they you, but no more cozying up to wild cats."

She said nothing, just looked at him over her bandana, trying to will away the aches and pains that thrummed through her body.

Seeing her wince, he shook his head, his voice rougher than usual. "I'm tabling this for now, but don't think this conversation is over."

"Don't ask me to be what I'm not," she rasped out.

He threw up his hand. "I'm not. I'm just asking you to temper that high courage and big heart."

"She didn't hurt me."

"But she could have. I can't lose you, Red."

And just like that, her anger disappeared and the world narrowed down to just the two of them. The cat and Charlie both lost in a mist. Even the pain had receded.

"I'll be careful."

"Uh, Boss."

"What, Charlie." Brandon's eyes never broke from

his wife's gaze.

"We're going to have company shortly."

Alex snapped back to the present and noticed the cat's screams had intensified. In the background, she could hear the shouts of men and the thudding of hooves.

"Stay and fight or cross over?" Charlie asked, his hand resting on his pistol.

"Cross. Get moving, O'Malley."

"You go, Brandon, so you can give us cover. Your better at distance shooting than I am." Her breath quickened as urgency coursed through her.

He didn't like it. She could see it in his eyes, but he understood the sense of it.

"See you on the other side, O'Malley." He urged Eagle across, not bothering to dismount. The rocky side of the mountain scraping the side of his leg with the roan's every step.

The buckskin whickered in distress as Eagle's hooves clopped on the narrow trail, leaving the mare behind.

"Your next, Charlie."

"I'm not doing it."

"Same goes. You're better with a long gun than I am. Please, Charlie." She all but wrung her hands.

"You're going to be the death of me, Young Alex." He started across, still in the saddle. His stirrup scraping rocks.

Brandon was already halfway across.

Both horses were setting a faster pace than they usually did on the narrow trail. The increased speed, ratcheting up the odds against them, making the dangerous crossing deadly. The drop on their left steep and leading to certain death.

Dancer's front hooves were on the Narrow Divide when the Comancheros burst into sight.

"There she is. Don't let her get away."

A shot went whizzing by her left ear.

"Shoot again and you die. I want her alive." Thiago's harsh voice rang out.

A man with a pockmarked face, and greasy hair showing under his cowboy hat, thumped his horse, leaned from his saddle and made a lunge for her. Then screamed in terror as a cat leaped from high overhead, knocking him from the saddle.

All hell broke loose.

Alex hooked her leg over her saddle to keep from knocking it against the rough outcropping and Dancer galloped onto the narrow trail. The Comancheros' horses panicked at the sight of the puma and began to buck and scream. A couple got the bit in their teeth and took off.

In the chaos, the buckskin disappeared.

Brandon fired over his shoulder.

Charlie did the same.

The puma went racing back up the hill, its tail lashing. Gunshots pinged off the walls near it, cascading rock and debris below.

Brandon made it to the other side before anyone was able to get their horse under control. Finally, one of the men wearing a colorful serape and riding a chestnut headed across the trail in pursuit.

Brandon fired.

The man dropped from the saddle and tumbled over the incline. The serape catching the wind as the Comanchero fell, looking like a giant, colorful bird as he floated out of sight.

Someone returned fire.

"I want the woman." *Woman. Woman. Woman,* echoed off the mountainside.

Charlie was now across.

The Comancheros stood on the other side watching as their quarry escaped their clutches.

Dancer had almost made it when a chunk of rock disappeared under his front left hoof. He bugled and rose on his hind legs. Alex clung as best she could with one leg in the stirrup and one wrapped around the saddle horn, her heart thundering, her pulse racing, and beads of icy sweat popping out on her forehead.

"We got this, boy." She spoke soothingly and lay a hand on his proud neck.

He nickered, came back down, and with tendons bunching, leaped the rest of the way across.

Before the horse had halted, Brandon scooped her out of the saddle and pressed her against him. His heart pounding.

"I'm okay."

He nodded and lay his forehead against hers.

The chestnut, that had been carrying the Comanchero, bumped against them as it came thundering across.

They broke apart.

"What do you think of saving that cat now?" she

teased, trying to get her breathing and racing heart under control.

"I'll never doubt you again." Then turned stone-cold serious. "I want you to do something for me. Promise me."

"What?" She stiffened. Whatever was coming she wasn't going to like it.

"I want you to head to the ranch without me."

"You can't ask that of me. I absolutely refuse. Besides, I have smallpox, he won't come within a hundred yards of me."

"He doesn't know that. With your bandana up and your hat down, wearing riding gloves, it's undetectable. And you're getting better every day. A couple of those scabs have fallen off."

"I'm not leaving you. End of discussion."

"He wants you, Alex. We've been down this road before. He's like Lavarah. He won't stop till he gets you or he's dead. I intend to make sure it's the latter."

"He doesn't even know me," she said, exasperation fighting hysteria. Frightened to death she'd lose this fight.

"You're a legend among the Comancheros. And I know men of Thiago's ilk. He'll be bucking to prove he's a better man than Lavarah. That he can take what Lavarah couldn't hold onto."

He looked across the Narrow Divide where the Comancheros waited on the other side.

He turned to Charlie. "I'm counting on you to get her safely home."

Charlie's expression grim, he gave a terse jerk of

his chin.

"I'm not going, Brandon."

"I want you plenty visible when you ride out of here. In fact, gallop out. They'll feel it's safe to cross and I'll pick them off."

"I'm not leaving." Her skin tightened as desperation built, slicking her nerves and coating her skin. The headache that her rushing blood had temporarily dispersed, surged back with a vengeance.

"Don't make me tie you on your saddle."

She whipped out her Peacemaker, determination riding her. "You aren't listening. I'm not going."

"Who are you going to shoot? Me or Charlie?" His eyes were patient above the bandana, knowing what he was asking of her. "Do you trust me?"

"With all my heart."

"Then go. I will come back to you."

"We do this together." Desperation and fear screamed through her.

"No, Red. Not this time."

"You can't ask me to do this, Brandon. You can't."

He bent down and kissed her through the bandanas they both wore then straightened. "I'll see you at the ranch."

He turned to his cowhand. "Get 'er done."

"Let's go, Young Alex." Charlie started toward her.

She turned the gun on Charlie. "Don't make me shoot you."

"If you didn't shoot me over that little ole garter snake," he referred to the snake he'd put in her boot back when she'd first joined up, "you ain't a gonna shoot me now."

"No. But I can make sure you sing soprano for a good long time," she threatened.

"I'd not enjoy that. But I agree with the Boss on this one." He took a step toward her. Her husband converged from the other side. She waved her gun back and forth between them.

"Alex." Brandon's voice soft.

She let the gun droop in her fingers and pleaded, "Don't ask this of me."

He took another step toward her. "I know this is so much harder than staying and fighting, but I can't be worrying about you and take out Thiago."

"You don't need to worry about me."

"Whether that's true or not I do, and will until I draw my last breath."

She looked into his eyes and read love and determination, and knew he spoke the truth.

Her breath came out in a jagged rush, grief keening through her, but she straightened her shoulders, looked him square in the eye and said as he had a moment before, "Then get 'er done."

She mounted Dancer, put heels to him, and didn't look back.

CHAPTER 31

Brandon stared after her. This is what he'd wanted, needed, to finish the job. To finish Thiago. The "I want the woman," echoing in his head, much like it had echoed on the mountainside, making his blood thunder in his ears as he clenched and unclenched his fists. Even so, watching her ride away left an emptiness that no amount of rightness filled.

"Good luck." Charlie strode to him, shook his hand and jumped on his horse.

"Take care of her."

"With my life." Charlie put heels to the piebald. The horse snorted and sidled then went plunging down the trail Dancer had disappeared on.

Brandon squared his shoulders, grabbed his rifle then crawled to the Narrow Divide. He dropped to the rocky ground, found a low boulder and waited.

An hombre started across. His stirrup scraped the side of the mountain. His mount spooked and nearly lost his footing as one hoof went over the edge, pebbles and shale clattering down the side, dropping into open space. The horse skittered backward and reared. When it came down, its rider hastily backed the animal onto solid ground, its hindquarters dancing from side to side.

Brandon continued to wait, his stomach in the dirt, his rifle barrel resting on the squat, gray-colored boulder.

A man, wearing a black sombrero with a silver band that glinted in the late afternoon sun, shouted orders. A different hombre saluted and started across on foot. He was nearly halfway across before Brandon raised his rifle, now sure of his shot, and fired. With a scream the man went tumbling into the abyss below.

Yelling and gunshots came across the divide, fired fast and at random. Most of them never reaching their destination. Hitting rocks and trees as they dropped through the air.

Brandon aimed at the black sombrero and fired.

"Damn."

As the other banditos ran for cover, Thiago stood his ground, just out of range.

The Comanchero leader bit out another sharp order. Firing ceased. He stared across the divide. Brandon swore he could see the hatred burning in the bandito's eyes. Well, that was okay with him. It was returned tenfold.

Finally, Thiago turned his back and shouted more orders. The men dismounted and began to break camp.

Impasse.

Brandon leaned his rifle against the bolder he'd used for cover, absently slapping at the dust built-up on the arm of his worn blue shirt, then settled in against the rough, grainy boulder. Instead of having his men picked off one by one, Thiago would send them for him at night. That's what he would do if he were in the Comanchero's shoes. Only if it were Brandon, he wouldn't send his men, he'd come himself.

While he waited, the sun slid toward the horizon, hitting the side of the mountain, turning rough gray rock to gleaming gold. As night fell, Brandon built a fire that crackled and threw off orange embers glowing against the dark. After he got it going, he stepped into the underbrush and waited. It wasn't long before he heard the clip-clop of a horse's hooves. Surprised that someone was riding or leading their horse across, he threw his rifle to his shoulder and, finger on the trigger, waited.

The fire threw the larger-than-life shadow of a horse that stepped into the campsite and nickered. Eagle whickered back.

The tension in his shoulders loosened. The dang buckskin. He didn't know whether to laugh or curse. The mare snorted and clomped right on up to Eagle who whickered in return. Just like an old married couple he thought as he settled back into the underbrush to wait.

It was after midnight when a man stole into camp.

Brandon fired. The hombre crumpled to the ground.

No one else came across.

The next night, Brandon picked off another Comanchero that had braved the Divide.

The third night Thiago sent three. Brandon was drifting in and out of sleep when Eagle whickered a warning. Shadowy figures sprang into the firelight. Brandon grabbed his Peacemaker and fired two shots in rapid succession before the third one leaped on him, his knife glittering in the tangerine glow of the campfire.

A sharp-edged rock bit into his shoulder and dust rose in a cloud, as the hombre, wiry and strong, knocked Brandon to the ground. The knife came arcing down. Moving at the last minute, the blade pricked Brandon's ear instead of his throat. With a sharp jab, he clouted the Comanchero on the side of the head. It stunned the man long enough for Brandon to roll him. The man fought fiercely and managed to flip him. Again, Brandon landed hard.

"The man you killed yesterday was my uncle." Drops of hot saliva landed on Brandon's face as the hombre spit out the words.

"Then maybe you should join him." Brandon grunted, managing to get a hand free and clock him on the jaw.

The hombre held on, the light of battle and hate glittering fiercely in his eyes. Knife still in hand, he sliced at Brandon. Again, Brandon managed to move at the last second, and the knife glanced off his sleeve.

They continued to roll and punch at each other, getting perilously close to the edge. Brandon felt air beneath his shoulder. The hombre's eyes glittered. "Maybe you can fly, yes?" He sneered.

"Maybe one of us can." Brandon gave a final shove and the man went screaming over the edge.

Bleeding in half a dozen places, Brandon pushed

to his feet. By his calculation, that should narrow the playing field down to four. As the moon dropped and the heavens turned from inky black to charcoal gray, he started across.

CHAPTER 32

She stared straight ahead. Even when the gunshot sounded she didn't look back, though a quiver traveled across her shoulders like cracking ice.

They rode till the sun sank below the horizon, turning the sky crimson in the process, before they stopped beside a stream.

A fire from twigs and branches pushed back the dark. With a handful of pine and oak at their backs, it was a near perfect campsite. Charlie had even managed to shoot an unsuspecting rabbit and fixed stew for supper.

An ember drifted towards Alex's tan canvas pants, then died and floated away.

There had been little conversation during the ride and less around the campfire. Charlie finished his coffee then broke the silence that hung heavy between them. "What's the plan, Young Alex?"

"What do you mean?" Alex stared at him, her eyes narrowing.

"We rode away and left your man to deal with a band of Comancheros. It's eating at you."

"And it's not you?" Fire burned behind her eyes and her words were delivered as rapid and hard as bullets.

"Of course, it is. But I see the need."

"You see the need to leave him behind?"

"I see the need to protect you."

"And if it weren't for me, you'd be back there fighting at his side." The words hung heavy and sad in the air.

"So, what's the plan? And it better be one I can live with."

"We give him another day. If he hasn't caught up with us by then we head back."

"That's not long enough. He can hold that spot at the end of the divide for weeks."

"Do you think they'll stick around that long?"

He shrugged.

"Two days."

"Four."

"Three."

He rubbed his whiskery jaw, the bristles making a whispering sound. "Alright. You realize he's either going to skin me or fire me, don't you?"

"I'll protect you or hire you back." She grinned at him.

"Counting on it."

CHAPTER 33

Night air hung heavy and still as Brandon traversed the Narrow Divide on foot, one hand on the stony wall at his side. Cool to the touch in spite of the night heat.

Behind him, pebbles rattled and pinged, bouncing down the mountainside. Someone or something was on the trail too.

Soundlessly he shifted, till his back pressed against the rocky surface of the mountainside, ignoring the sharp protruding edge poking against his shoulder as he strained to hear. His vision unable to pierce the black. Tension riding him, he waited.

The rattling of pebbles stopped. Nothing broke the stillness.

Still, he waited.

Slowly, the tightness in his shoulders loosened. Whatever was back there meant him no harm.

Once again, he started forward. His boot heels crunching loose shale. He stopped once to listen.

Nothing.

Quietly, he strode forward, close enough to see the orange glow of the campfire and hear the murmurings of the men and the strident hectoring of their leader.

Brandon's lips curved in a cold smile. Thiago was not happy.

He inched closer, staying in the shadows as he drew his gun.

Thiago stood with his back to Brandon, dressing down his men. Hands on hips, anger quivering in his voice.

"Thiago," Brandon called out.

Gun in hand, the Comanchero whirled. So did the three remaining hombres who followed him.

The roar of bullets sounded as Thiago and Brandon fired simultaneously.

Thiago's gun dropped from limp fingers and he keeled over as pain seared Brandon's side.

Shots rang out behind him.

One hombre grabbed his shoulder, another his leg. The third looked around wildly and ran for his horse. Jumping on its bare back, he galloped away. The other two went limping after him, disappearing into the shadows.

Alex and Charlie strode into the firelight.

Brandon heaved a sigh and let his Colt drop to his side. "Red. Red. Red. What am I going to do with you?"

"Considering we just—" Her hot, snapping eyes dropped to his side where blood dripped from between his fingers. "Brandon." She hurtled toward him, tripping over a rock then righting herself. She shoved his hand away. "Let me see."

"I'm okay."

"I'll be the judge of that.

"Charlie, see if you can find a clean rag, whiskey

and a canteen filled with water."

"Yes, ma'am."

Charlie strode over and rifled through the saddle bags that lay with the saddles around the campfire.

"Sit," Alex commanded.

Since his side ached like the devil and the blood loss was making him lightheaded, he did as he was told and dropped to the ground, leaning against a nearby log that had been pulled up to the ember circle. Manfully biting back a groan.

Alex started to tug his shirt over his head then dropped it like a hot potato and backed up.

"Charlie," she called, her voice strained, clenching and unclenching her hands.

With quick long strides, Charlie was back beside her, holding a canteen, a bottle of whiskey and clean rags.

"I don't dare touch him," she said through strained lips.

"Not to worry. This ain't my first rodeo."

Charlie poured water over one of the rags and began to swab Brandon's blood-soaked side. Brandon bit off a groan, but he couldn't stop the quiver that ran along his skin at the pain.

Seeing it, Alex bit her lips, her features drawn and tight.

"Boss, I need you to turn toward the campfire to get a better look at that hole in your side." Alex flinched as Charlie stuck a finger in the mangled flesh.

"Ouch. Dammit, Charlie."

Without a word, Charlie handed him the whiskey.

Brandon took a healthy swig and subsided.

"The bullet's still in there."

Even in the rosy glow of the campfire, Alex's face took on a greenish hue.

Brandon took another healthy gulp of the whiskey. "Get to it then."

Charlie pulled out his four-inch folding knife and dipped it in the fire then went to work on torn flesh.

Brandon white-knuckled the log as Charlie probed. Alex's face went from green to white then back to green again. With each movement of the knife, white-hot pain leapt up Brandon's side and he cursed under his breath.

"I found it. You're going to have to hold steady, Boss."

His hands clenching tufts of straggly grass, Brandon grunted to keep from screaming like a girl as Charlie dug under the bullet and flipped it out. It rolled on the ground, shiny, wet and red.

Alex took a few steps back, turned her back and heaved.

Charlie poured whiskey on a cloth, wiped Brandon's side with it, then wrapped the strips around Brandon's waist.

"Guess it's time to clean up camp then see if they've got any food in their saddlebags." Charlie grabbed Thiago's limp body by his boots and heaved it over the side of the mountain.

As Charlie came back, Brandon pushed to his feet. "Collect what you can then we better head on back to the other side in case anybody decides to return for their leader."

Alex bit back a protest. She pushed out a whistly breath and gave a sharp jerk of her chin.

Charlie did a quick, thorough search, tossed a couple of saddlebags over his shoulder and came back. "Let's go."

Brandon carefully pushed to his feet.

"I'll go first," Alex said and started across.

"After you, Boss."

Brandon went next, followed by Charlie, knowing they were doing their best to protect him. It rankled. He should be taking care of them. Taking care of his wife and his crew was his job. No one else's.

They proceeded slowly. Cautiously. The night quiet and cool.

Alex had made it to the other side of the Divide when the ledge beneath Brandon's left boot crumbled. Rocks, pebbles and dirt went flying down into the nothingness below. Weak with loss of blood and pain, he lost his balance and slipped. He grabbed frantically for purchase as he went tumbling over the side.

"Brandon," Alex screamed.

He grabbed out with his hands and managed to catch the edge of the ridge with his fingertips while his boots kicked air.

She grabbed his arms and held on. Her toes scraped rock as his weight pulled her forward.

"O'Malley, let go." Fear juddered through him.

"Never."

"Let go, dammit." His feet scraped against the cliff wall, trying frantically to find a toehold.

"I got you, Boss." Charlie's voice quiet, he lay on the trail. Reaching out he grasp the arm closest to him and began to haul Brandon up. Brandon dug in with his fingers and pushed with his toes, his weight no longer dragging on O'Malley.

As they tugged and he pushed, Brandon came slithering over the edge.

Charlie grunted as one of Brandon's boots made contact with his nose. On hands and knees, Brandon crawled till he hit the widened trail and rolled over on his back, his chest heaving.

Charlie slithered on his stomach. As he reached open ground beyond the choke point, Brandon and O'Malley grabbed him by the shoulders and pulled him the rest of the way.

Somehow, all three made it to safety.

Now that the danger was over, pain came screaming back, his side bleeding like a stuck pig. He stood up, taking stock of himself, his wife and his friend. O'Malley pushed to her feet and barreled into his arms.

"I nearly lost you." She shuddered.

He ripped down her bandana and kissed her. A long, hard kiss of thanksgiving.

She pushed away. "What in Sam Hill are you doing!" She thrust her bandana back up.

He touched her head and asked in mock concern, "Have you taken a blow to the head, O'Malley? You've forgotten what a kiss is?"

Charlie snorted.

"Are you trying to kill yourself?"

"Your bumps are all gone," he said gently as the moon came out of hiding to shine full on her face. "You're cured, O'Malley."

"No, Brandon. I still have a dozen or so that aren't visible," she muttered backing up.

Be that as it may, it had been too damn long since he kissed his wife. He didn't regret that kiss for a minute. Surely, nothing that pleasurable could bring misery and death. But he dropped his arms, knowing she was right. He turned to Charlie, who'd also gotten to his feet.

Charlie threw out his arms. "Don't feel the need to kiss me, Boss."

Swaying slightly, Brandon chuckled.

"Sit," his wife commanded. "Charlie, redress his wound, he's bleeding again. I'll build a fire."

Brandon dropped to the ground, leaning against the boulder that sat at the edge of the trail where it widened.

While Alex built a fire, Charlie redressed Brandon's wound then made coffee. The nutty, earthy aroma had Brandon's nose quivering. Next, the cowpuncher opened a can of peaches with his knife and held it out to Brandon, whose stomach growled in response.

"Where did we get these?" Brandon asked around a mouthful as he dug into the juicy, yellow-fleshed fruit with the fork Charlie provided.

"Courtesy of the Comancheros." Charlie grinned and held up a bulging saddle bag. "Got one for you too, Young Alex."

Her face lit up and her Adam's apple bobbed as she

swallowed pooling saliva. "Got one for yourself?"

"I do. And that will finish the peaches." He handed her a can he'd opened and a fork.

"We got anything else?" she asked around a mouthful.

"We got beans, tomaters, condensed milk, apples, and corned beef. Some in tin cans. Some in glass jars. Tomorrow night I'll go hunting then fix us a stew and maybe dole out those apples."

"Those Comancheros eat better than we do. Probably stole it all," she grumbled.

Charlie nodded in agreement then handed out jerky and hardtack.

Brandon promptly dunked the hardtack in his peach juice.

"Kinda makes you long for Cookie's homemade peach pie, don't it?" Charlie said.

Brandon laughed then grimaced. "When we get home that's the first thing I'm going to ask him to bake."

"Not me. I'm going to ask for cinnamon rolls." Alex wore a dreamy expression.

"Yeah, I vote for cinnamon rolls too. Though his peach pie is mighty tasty," Charlie said.

Alex scooted over by Brandon and he threw his arm around her. Luckily, she was on his good side or that pleasure would be denied. She leaned against him for a moment, then moved reluctantly away. They all sat in companionable silence watching the flames shoot up and light the night sky, listening to the crackle of the embers.

A log snapped and popped loud in the night like a pistol shot, making him reach for his Peacemaker.

"It's just burning wood." Alex arched her eyebrows.

"Yeah, guess I haven't gotten used to no one taking pot shots at us yet," he joked.

Still, he gave an uneasy look around, cold fingers of trepidation crawling up and down his spine. Thiago might be dead, but it wasn't over. He could sense it, feel it. Almost taste it in the air.

CHAPTER 34

Brandon's unease transferred to Alex.

She glanced over her shoulder, fighting the weariness that dogged her even after a two-day rest, and turned her attention to her husband, studying him from beneath her ancient, wide-brimmed cowboy hat that shadowed her features.

Oh, he acted relaxed enough, joking, riding easy in the saddle in spite of his wound. Still, she knew him. As well as she knew herself. Picked up on the way his sharp eyes were always checking their surroundings or looking over his shoulder when he thought no one was paying attention. The way his mouth momentarily tightened before he caught himself and relaxed it. Or the twitch of his shoulders. The way he rode with his hand on his gun. Casual things, but they added up to worry. And whatever was on his mind, he wasn't sharing it with her or Charlie.

"Want to tell me what's wrong?" She reined Dancer alongside Eagle and tried again.

"What makes you think anything is wrong?" He rode with one hand holding the reins and one hand on his thigh, near his gun, comfortable in the saddle as the big roan trotted through scrub, cactus and sand, kicking up fine clouds of grit beneath broad hooves.

Push it or let it go?

For a moment, she gave him look for look then dropped her gaze along with her shoulders. "Alright, Wade. I suppose you'll tell me when you're ready." Alex kicked Dancer lightly and he broke into a lope leaving the roan behind. She was too dang tired to argue with him. Her back ached and her scabs itched. She scratched her arm and felt one loosen.

Hooves pounded behind her then Brandon reined in alongside.

"I can't tell you what's wrong because I don't know. It's just a feeling I can't shake. I think we're being followed, but I've seen no signs of another human being behind us."

She looked behind her. And saw nothing. Still... "I trust your feelings. They've never steered you wrong. We'll keep a sharp eye out."

He gave her a smile that had her heartbeat picking up and her insides softening. It had been like that since the first moment she saw him striding toward her, a purpling sunset at his back. Would it be like that in ten years? Twenty? More? Somehow, she thought so.

"What's got that smile playing about your lips, O'Malley?"

She leaned over in her saddle and whispered in his ear then winked as color rose up his collar and flooded his features.

"What a mouth you have." He twitched in his saddle as if trying to get comfortable.

She grinned, satisfied.

"It's your own fault you know. If you weren't so good in the sack."

"O'Malley." He frowned and threw a quick glance at Charlie who was trying mighty hard to pretend he hadn't heard anything and might have pulled it off if his lips weren't twitching.

Brandon put heels to the roan and galloped away, clearly leaving the victory to his wife.

As the day progressed, their pace slowed. The sun beat down hot and oppressive, heat gleaming off the mountains in the distance. Their horses' hoof prints scattered by a stiff, hot breeze.

Alexandria's faded green cotton shirt stuck damply to her shoulders. The buckskin trod behind, occasionally breaking into a trot to catch up with Eagle and clip-clop beside him. Charlie and Alex chuckled. Wade just shook his head.

The buckskin had just pulled alongside the stallion when a jackrabbit hopped under the mare's nose, causing the horse to snort and dance to the side, right into a gray-green, tree-height Devil's Cactus, with a branching trunk. The needles shot out in a silvery-shimmer, embedding in the horse's right flank. Screaming in pain, the mare reared and galloped off. Hooves thudding. Throwing sand.

All three went tearing after the panicked animal. It was Eagle's bugling call that had the mare slowing, swaying from side to side, trying to dislodge the intense torment.

Wade's rope sang out, stilled in the air, then

dropped over the horse's head. The buckskin screamed and reared.

Dancer drew alongside. Alex's stomach flopped. Over a dozen spines protruded from the mare's flank. Alex leaped out of the saddle and reached for the bridle.

"Be careful, O'Malley."

She ignored him and began to sooth the mare. When the mare had calmed and stood quivering she glanced at Brandon and read the speculation in his eyes.

"Don't even think it, Wade. We aren't shooting her."

"It might be the kindest thing."

She glanced at the mare's swelling belly. "Eagle might not take kindly to the mare and his colt being put down."

Wade took a good look at the horse's belly and began to swear, ending with, "What do you want me to do?"

"Get a fire going, heat your knife and give it to me.

"Charlie, gather some yucca root and make a paste."

The men didn't bother to argue, just went about their assigned tasks. In a short period of time, Wade had built a fire and heated his knife.

"You want me to do it?" You didn't spend time in the Southwest without learning how to remove spines.

She almost said yes.

Then straightened her shoulders and swallowed,

her throat dry. "I'll do it."

Wade went to the buckskin's head and held it, talking cowboy-speak in a low, soothing voice. The mare nuzzled his chest. Alex shook her head and muttered, "Even lady horses."

Wade gave a snort much like the horse.

She took a deep breath, pinched the nearest spine close to its base and, using the knife and her forefinger, pulled it out.

Hindquarters shifting, the mare screamed, stomping about. Alex jumped nimbly back.

"Charlie," Wade bellowed, worry in his eyes, his lips tight.

Charlie dropped the roots by the fire, but before he could stride to the mare to grab the other side of the bridle, Eagle clomped forward and butted the mare's neck. The mare quieted.

"Make it snappy, O'Malley."

Sweat built on her forehead. It was dicey pulling the spikes out without them breaking off when the horse started moving around. Somehow, she managed. Two down, many to go.

She wiped her forehead and kept working. At some point, the mare had quit moving about, just whickered pitifully whenever a spine came out. Alex found it more painful to listen to than to jump out of the way when the mare pranced around from the pain.

Finally, she squeezed the last spike and jerked it out. She stood panting, right along with the horse.

"Go get yourself a drink of water or something

stronger. I'll slather this on." Charlie nudged her out of the way.

She nodded and stumbled away. She hadn't even seen him standing there. Sand danced in the air as she thumped down on the ground and reached for her canteen, glugging thirstily.

A few minutes later, the two men came striding up.

"You done good, Young Alex," Charlie said.

"Of course, she did," Brandon added, winking at her.

"Seeing its suppertime, I'll fix us some vittles."

She looked up in surprise. Sure enough, the sun, low on the horizon, had turned the sky a fiery red, adding a glow to the buckskin's unique coloring. Alex sighed and leaned back against a sandy brown, squat boulder.

Charlie threw everything they had on her plate. Beans, tomatoes, apples, corned beef and hardtack.

"Thanks, Charlie," she said around a mouthful of beans. "This is a veritable feast."

"You earned it, kid."

She glanced over at the horses nibbling at the occasional sprout of grass protruding between rough rocks and munching on saltbrush, sagebrush, mesquite leaves and whatever woody plants they could find. The mare was quiet. The setting sun fell on the raised welts, slathered with the yucca poultice Charlie had made. The buckskin nudged its sore flank, snorted, then went back to nibbling at a feathery-looking, grayish-green mesquite leaf.

Alex nodded to herself. The mare was going to be okay. Her stomach growled and she turned her attention to her tin plate and began wolfing down the contents.

"Whoa, O'Malley. Slow down before you choke," her loving husband told her.

She glared at him as she masticated, swallowed, then took another mouthful. Finally, when she was sure she couldn't eat another bite, she set her plate on the ground.

"Want some more coffee, Young Alex?" Both Charlie and Brandon squatted on the other side of the fire, its flames licking upward, crackling cheerily in the quiet.

She glanced toward them then let out a blood-curdling scream as a demon straight from hell came racing toward them.

CHAPTER 35

"Look out." Leaping to her feet, she yanked out her Colt then tripped over a log, as she was about to fire. The shot went wild.

On a gray-dappled gelding, Thiago thundered toward them. His features swollen, dried blood covering his face and shirt, his eyes wild with hate and pain.

He raised his gun and aimed it straight at her, screaming, "Watch your whore die." He fired just as Alex rolled. The shot hit the log Alex had tripped over. The bullet embedded in it, splitting the wood with a piercing crack, as chips of bark flew.

Brandon got off a shot, but Thiago slipped to the side, riding low on his horse, coming straight for her. Charlie fired, but missed, as Thiago jumped from the stallion. Tossing his gun aside, he whipped out a wicked-looking knife.

He landed on her, knife raised. The long, serrated blade gleaming in the firelight. Her head thumped against hard earth. Alex pushed back with all her strength and he went flying backwards. She blinked in surprise then realized Brandon had jumped him and his momentum had carried them both off of her. They rolled on the ground, perilously near the fire.

Thiago slashed out with the knife.

Alex bit back a gasp as blood erupted from Brandon's forearm. She rushed toward Thiago and tried to pull him off. He fought with the strength of the insane and flung her back.

"Charlie, keep her back," Brandon bit out.

She fought Charlie as he grabbed her, but his arms went round her and locked her in a grip she couldn't break.

"Don't distract him," he said in a low voice.

She subsided.

Flashing in the firelight, the knife came down again.

Brandon deflected it at the last moment. It slid along the front of his shirt, exposing flesh and a thin streak of blood. Brandon flipped Thiago. Thiago pushed upward with his knife, hate burning in his eyes like living coals.

They grappled. The knife going towards Brandon, then Thiago, then Brandon again. With a move quick as a cat's, Brandon snatched the knife.

"No one threatens my wife, you son of a jackal." He plunged the wicked blade into Thiago's hate-filled heart.

The Comanchero's eyes rolled back and he lay still.

Charlie dropped his arms and Alex raced toward Brandon sobbing as he pushed slowly and painfully to his feet.

"Are you alright?" Tears streamed down her face. Her heart thundered like a wild thing caught in a trap.

"Yeah, Red. Just flesh wounds. Nothing deep." He

pushed the hair that had tumbled around her face away and drew her to him, dropping a kiss on top of her head. The warmth of his arms stole over her, calming her, slowing her rapidly beating heart, while speeding up the blood racing through her veins.

Finally, he let her go. "Gad, that bastard was hard to kill. He must have landed on a ledge."

Charlie thrust a bottle at him. He took several quick gulps then pushed it back to his cowhand. Charlie took a gulp and passed it to Alexandria, who poured some in her cup, took a quick glug and came up coughing.

Charlie grabbed the Comanchero by his boots and dragged him into the underbrush. He rounded up Thiago's gelding and took off the saddle and bridle. The gelding snorted and joined the others.

"Well, I gotta say, it's never dull around you two," Charlie said as he settled back against a smooth-barked desert willow and calmly reached for his coffee.

CHAPTER 36

Four days later.

"There it is. The Rio Grande." Charlie, leading the gray-dappled gelding, pulled up alongside Alex and Brandon, and pointed at the mighty stretch of water. Yellow and blue serrated skies, and sandy orange mountains mirrored in its sparkling silvered depths.

The buckskin, still favoring its left flank, limped behind.

Excitement zitted through Brandon sending his blood racing. Across the Rio lay Texas and home. He wanted his family whole again. To see his children. He glanced at Alex and caught the same intense longing on her lovely features as she stared across the river. She never spoke of it, never complained, but he knew if anything, she missed her babes even more than he did.

Alex turned her head. The longing disappeared and excitement flashed in amber eyes. "So, what are we waiting for?"

"Not a thing." He raised his reins and gave her a wink then nudged Eagle. The stallion went splashing into the water, droplets of liquid color rising in the air.

"See ya on the other side." Alexandria's voice rang out as the big black danced past Brandon's roan, splashing them in the process, sending droplets plopping then dripping from the brim of Brandon's hat.

Leaning forward, he kept a close watch as Alex's stallion began to swim, tendons flexing. Strong legs striking outward. Fighting the river as liquid churned.

He heard a splash and whicker from behind. Glancing back, he saw the piebald and dappled-gray trot into the water.

"Undertow," Alex called over her shoulder before turning her attention to the current and her horse fighting it. Brandon divided his attention between the river and O'Malley as the water whooshed past. He was now at its center, waves dancing around him. Dancer was gaining ground, drawing closer and closer to shore. With a heave, the stallion pulled out of the water, hooves slipping on the steep, slick bank, before it found its footing and went galloping up the wet slope.

Alexandria let out a rebel yell and exuberantly waved her worn, tan hat—a bullet hole in its crown—in the air.

Grinning widely, he turned his attention to his own mount, now deep in the current that was trying to carry them downstream, helping Eagle with heels and hands. The bank grew closer. Then they were in the shallows. The roan's hooves making sucking sounds as they left the water. He angled his mount to the right, avoiding the torn up slick surface Dancer had charged up. Rocks slithered under Eagle's hooves as the horse went clambering up it, slipping backwards a few yards before it bunched its muscles and leaped up the bank throwing clods of red mud behind it.

Again, O'Malley whooped and waved her hat.

Brandon's mouth muscles stretched from cheek to cheek. He gave her a mile-wide smile, took off his hat and dipped it in her direction then shoved it back on his head and turned his attention to his cowhand nearing the belly of the river.

The piebald and the dappled-gray were swimming strongly. The buckskin grumbling in the shallows on the opposite shore, putting one hoof tentatively in front of the other. Wade shook his head. Other than a brood mare, the hoss was next to useless.

As if to bely his thoughts, the buckskin leaped into the water, prism-colored droplets cascading around it.

His attention veered back to his cowhand. Charlie's mount and the gray had hit the center of the river where the current was the strongest. Dark waves rose and lapped at them, sending them backwards, toward the shore they'd just left.

Alex, who had ridden up beside him, stiffened.

"Charlie can handle the horses and the current," Brandon said.

"Yes. Yes, he can."

But he heard the hoarse in her voice and saw the tightening of her mouth. Her eyes fixed on the rider fighting his way across.

The horse paddled in place, throwing up great sheets of water. The liquid throwing rainbows in the glare of the sun. The beauty at odds with the danger.

"Lean forward, Charlie, lean forward."

As if hearing her, the rider leaned forward.

"He knows what he's doing," Brandon said calmly, forcing his hands, tight around the saddle pommel, to loosen.

"I know."

She straightened and gathered her reins.

"Don't even think about it, Red. If he comes loose from that saddle, I'll go in."

She threw him an outraged glare.

"You're good, but I've got the muscle."

She subsided grumbling.

Charlie's horse broke free from the current and throwing out long, sinewed legs began to swim strongly towards shore. The gray alongside, the buckskin determinedly behind it.

Then they were in the shallows.

Three yards from the bank.

Two.

One.

The horse came slithering up the slick incline, kicking rocks in its wake. The gelding behind it and the buckskin behind the gelding.

A large gray rock loosened.

A Western diamondback came slithering out, angry and spitting. Six feet long with diamond-shaped blotches, and black and white bands near the tail.

Before the creature could reach the horse, Alex drew and fired. The snake's head spun in the air, near the horse's nose. The horse reared unseating Charlie, who went flying over the back of the dappled gelding behind him, brushing against the buckskin who, with hooves flailing, skittered out of his way. He hit the ground with a thud, his head glancing off a protruding, damp rock and lay still, his arm in the shallows.

"Charlie," Alex screamed.

Both Alex and Brandon leapt out of their saddles and went running toward the motionless cowboy.

Alex reached him first and wiped his face with her damp sleeve. "Charlie. Charlie, can you hear me?"

His eyes opened. "Mighty fine shooting, Young Alex." His head dropped to the side, his eyes closed and his mouth fell open as unconsciousness claimed him.

CHAPTER 37

Huff.

Alex's lungs burned as they hauled Charlie up the bank, her muscles screaming, her boots squishing in the mud. He weighed more than she would have expected for such a wiry man. With a sucking sound, they yanked him out of the muck and onto a bed of cushiony, greenish-brown grass.

Brandon made a fire and broke camp, while Alexandria saw to Charlie.

"Next time he comes round, get some of this down him." Brandon shoved a flask at her.

After wiping his face again and calling his name several times, Charlie's lids flickered.

She held his head. "Here have some of this."

"Wouldn't turn it down," he rasped. He took a gulp, coughed, then took another. He pushed up on an elbow, crumpled, then with a determined grunt, managed to sit up. Looking at the sky deepening into orange and a purplish blue, he said, "Looks like we can get another hour of riding in."

Alexandria pushed on his shoulder and he subsided way too easy to her way of thinking. "We're making camp. I'm worn out."

"Mmhmm. I know you're champing at the bit to get home and see your young'uns."

"An hour isn't going to make that much difference, Charlie." Though, her heart was wild with the need to see her babies. They were now in Texas, just days away from Silverhills. She wanted nothing more than to jump on Dancer and ride for home as hard and fast as her mighty steed would go. But she couldn't, wouldn't, sacrifice a friend to do it.

"Well, I can at least see to the horses. They made it alright?" He looked around.

Some color had come back in Charlie's face, though the skin still stretched tight over bone and had a gray shade to it. Dark rings circled his eyes.

Alexandria jerked a thumb to her right. Only the pinto was tethered. The gelding could go or stay, as far as they were concerned, and nothing short of a cattle prod would get the buckskin to leave Eagle. And Eagle and Dancer weren't going anywhere.

"For a moment there, I thought that buckskin was going to slither right back into the water or kick me in the head. I'm relieved she managed to avoid both."

Handing him a tin filled with stew from last night's leftovers, and a cup of coffee, he'd liberally spiked with whiskey, Brandon said, "Good thing for her. As hard as your head is it might have split her hoof. I'm just surprised there wasn't a dent in that rock you landed on."

Charlie grinned and took a gulp of coffee. "Right fine coffee." He toasted Brandon with it.

Brandon chuckled and handed a cup and plate to

Alex.

"Is this one doctored too?" She looked at the tin cup suspiciously and sloshed it around.

"Figured you could use it."

She took a careful sip. After the burning subsided the glow set in. "Trying to get me drunk?"

"And if I am?"

"I'd say it's working." She grabbed her tin, filled with stew, and began to eat with gusto.

The sky darkened, stars came out diamond bright and a full moon shone down on the clearing. The burning firewood crackled and popped, throwing orange embers into the sky.

Charlie sat down his plate and burrowed into his blanket. His mouth open, he was soon making soft snorting noises.

She looked at Brandon sitting across from her and he looked at her. He scooped up his blanket and shoved it under his arm. "I notice you aren't wearing your mask."

"The last scab dropped off."

"I thought as much. Care to take a walk by the river?" His gaze holding hers, he pushed to his feet and held out his hand.

They were close enough to the water she could hear the gentle ripple of waves lapping against rock.

Her insides warmed and her blood leaped, but all she said was, "What about, Charlie?"

"He's sleeping like a baby."

The snorting sounds turned to a full out snore.

"I rest my case."

"What about your knife wounds?"

"I barely feel them. Though, I'm not averse to you kissing them and making them better."

"Well, it has been a while since we've walked along the river."

"Much too long for my liking."

"And mine." She took his hand and they strolled into the dark.

CHAPTER 38

Leather creaked and wind whispered.

The horses loped through rustling grasses rooted on rolling prairies and around scattered mesquites with feathery, fern-like leaves.

They had been traveling for seven days. Not pushing it, but not lolly-gagging either.

Alex's blood quickened when they broke free of the wide grasslands and entered Hill Country, crossing spring-fed rivers and climbing craggy limestone hills. Riding under majestic juniper and oak, with wide, spreading branches cooling the ground and giving shade from the scorching sun.

They stopped on a rise covered with Blackfoot daisy and silvery Texas sage. The sun hit the foothills on the other side, sending flashes of silver from the granite in the mountains.

Below them a busy ranch beckoned.

A ranch hand glanced up, caught sight of them and began to holler. People poured out of buildings and corrals.

Mongrel began to bark. Tail waving madly, tongue hanging out, the dog came racing up the hill.

As he'd done on another occasion Jeff jumped on a

mount and galloped forward to meet them.

Jon and Marie waved chubby arms in the air and trotted down the road in their direction.

Alex's eyes filled, right along with her heart. She put heels to Dancer's sides. He reared, gave a loud bugle, and bunching sinewy muscles, went leaping down the hill, with Brandon and Charlie close behind. The spare horses trotted after them, as the threesome raced headlong toward a ranch called Silverhills.

At last, they were home.

AUTHOR'S NOTE

Just a little historical trivia—in no particular order:

People in the Old West used willow bark for pain and fever. Willow bark contains salicin which acts like aspirin to reduce pain and fever. The bark could be chewed on or made into a tea.

The term zitted means to move quickly, much as we use zipped today.

Hardtack is hard biscuits.

Commercial canning started in the U.S. in 1812.

The Narrow Divide is strictly of the author's making.

Cowboys referred to Jumping Cholla as Devil's Cactus for its nasty habit of launching its barbed spines into tender flesh.

In 1873, the Peacemaker, i.e. Colt Single Action Army, was introduced to the Wild West, where it gained immense popularity. A single action revolver, it held six cartridges in a revolving cylinder. The cartridges metallic.

Smallpox inoculations did exist during the 1800s, but weren't always readily available in sparsely populated areas of the Old West and Mexico.

Coffee sold for fifteen to twenty-five cents a

pound.

Flannel and wool shirts were sometimes worn year-round, but cotton and linen were preferred in the summer.

If you'd like more cowboy trivia, you can find it at: https://cowboytrivia.blogspot.com/

ABOUT SANDRA

Sandra, who writes as both S. Cox and Sandra Cox, is an animal lover and avid gardener. She spent a number of years in the Midwest chasing down good Southern BBQ. By the time she moved to North Carolina where Southern BBQ is practically a staple, she'd become a vegetarian.

She and her husband are ruled by four cats and a dog. An award-winning author, her stories consist of all things Western and more.

Sandra can be found at:

https://sandracoxwriter.com

OR https://cowboytrivia.blogspot.com

OR https://sandracox.blogspot.com

If you'd like notification of new releases, I invite you to sign up on the contact/newsletter form at *sandracoxwriter* or *sandracox.blogspot* (addies above). Just type in NEW RELEASE. Her twitter handle is: Sandra_Cox and her Amazon page is https://www.amazon.com/stores/Sandra-Cox/author/B002BM3AKC

Last but not least, if you enjoyed this story enough

to leave a good review, thank you so much. Great reviews are an author's bread, butter and favorite ice cream, all rolled up in one.